A MILLION LIVES

D1519347

LAURA KOSTWINDER

FriesenPress

Suite 300 - 990 Fort St
Victoria, BC, V8V 3K2
Canada

www.friesenpress.com

ISBN
978-1-5255-7444-3 (Hardcover)
978-1-5255-7445-0 (Paperback)
978-1-5255-7446-7 (eBook)

1. FICTION, FAIRY TALES, FOLK TALES, LEGENDS & MYTHOLOGY

Distributed to the trade by The Ingram Book Company

For my teacher Mrs. Longpré who believed in me, and my father who gave me courage. But above all, to my mother, who inspired me to accept myself and flourish.

CHAPTER ONE:

THE DAUGHTER
OF DARKNESS

First, there was Adam... then there was Eve.

In the beginning, God created beauty and all that was good. He created the Heavens and the Earth and creatures of many kinds. There was harmony and peace and then...He created *them*. He gave living beings everything they would ever need, yet they always sought more. In time, they would learn that everything comes with a price. But back then, they were foolish and wanted to know why; why they couldn't be like God, not knowing it was all a lie.

She breathed her first breath of life. She was born and she knew why. They were the chosen ones and they were the first. He was the day and she was the night. He was man and she was woman, because from his rib bone she became alive. They walked together infinitely, but they were not alone, for the Heavenly Father was with them and loved them more than they could have ever known.

Her Father was the perfect image of purity and love. He was the light, and they basked in the warmth and protection of being so close to the sun. He gave them the freedom to do whatever they pleased, except to stay far away from this one, single tree. They were complete and they had all they would ever need. Nothing would ever harm them, for they were free from evil things.

Sitting in the tall spears of soft, green grass, they could gaze upon the mountains of the Garden of Eden, a sacred place known to no more than two. Everything was alive, and all salient animals lived in harmony, peace.

In Paradise, elephants and lions could be seen eating together from the tender fruit of billowing bushes; families of small ducks could waddle toward the gentle waves of the quiet stream without any fear of being attacked. The wind spoke in soft, gentle tones, and the water splashed playfully if anyone got too close.

Here in this land of love, fire would tickle and not burn, and terrible natural disasters never occurred. The dark soil was rich in nutrients, and the trees grew tall and produced the epitome of luscious fruit.

Eve had a curious mind; one filled with compassion and joy, but curious all the same. She loved her father dearly, but often questioned His intentions. She, like many more to come, would question how a being with so much power could be capable of a love so simple and pure. A mystery, her father was indeed. An enigma, or a puzzle to be solved, yet impossible to fully understand.

Her God was beyond being incredible; her God was the epitome of astounding goodness and sacredness. Love is the most powerful motivator, and it drives people to care so deeply for others that they would sacrifice anything to save them, even themselves. Unfortunately for many, clouded judgement distorts decisions made based on love.

Adam and Eve were pure as well, made in His image and born out of the dust of this beautiful land. Eve knew this with all of her heart, yet she still understood that the potential for darkness was far from nonexistent. Because they were of the flesh, and not entirely in spirit, they were susceptible to the temptations of darkness. In the beginning, she rarely breathed a word of this to Adam, as she feared a betrayal—or worse, a loss. However, in time she began to see that he too was like her, a human.

They kept it to themselves, never forgetting, but still wondering if anyone would ever understand the struggle that came with being an "angel" in a world full of perfect morals. It was difficult at times, observing the perfection of the world, knowing that in a single moment they could destroy it all. They both had the potential for sin, and wickedness, despite living in a perfect world. And yes, to Eve, the purity and perfection of it all was almost, at times, too surreal. After all, what is right without wrong, or light without darkness?

To Eve, life was a mystery, a journey, and an adventure. She sought to live life to its great ever-fulfilling potential, and learn lessons that could only be achieved through fault and failure. She wished to gaze at the sky, and run with the wind, without the need to return home after dark. She knew the day, and wished to see the night, for she knew it had beauty of its own. The stars shone ever so brightly in the hours of darkness, and she too wished to be free to shine in the midst of the twilight.

It was not until she surrendered herself to the infinite possibilities of life that she opened herself up to darkness. She did not know what evil was, as she had never experienced it in her life. Darkness lurks and is found in many of the unhappiest of places, often further within ourselves rather than surrounding us from all sides.

She was pure love and was shielded for so long; never understanding what sin truly meant. That was before she met *him*. But it had to happen, despite all that would follow.

At the darkest hour her eyes were opened, and she began to follow a very different path, one that diverged widely from the one she was seemingly destined to follow. It led her to the tree, the tenacious Tree of Knowledge.

His name was Lucifer, bearer of light, the morning star; and her downfall. He showed her a different type of world, one where she could be more like God, have more power. His claims were justified, and his case was well-defended. Surely, the words spoken must've been the truth. After all, who could fathom the guilt of lying so plainly and contently? Adam made his choice as well, fully embracing the opportunity, believing in the innocence of good intentions and advice. All they had to do was eat this luscious, tender, forbidden fruit, blossoming from the scraggly branches of the massive tree.

To think and never do would be controversial to the art of progress. So, they took the fruit and held it in their hands. As their teeth broke through the fragile flesh of the fruit, they suddenly knew the terrible implications of their decision.

Her name was Eve, a name that meant to be living, but today, she had died.

CHAPTER TWO:
A FLOOD OF TEARS

It was not long after the fall of Adam and Eve that others were born into this new world, far from the paradise that had been a privilege. First came Cain and Abel, the possessed spirit and the breathing spirit, who could not be similar. Not so unlike the disloyalty shown by his forebears, Cain was filled with an evil spirit so powerful and full of malice and spite that he was overcome with a desire for revenge.

He acted upon enmity, and cruelly murdered his flesh and blood with his own hands, tainted hands. Years later, the world had spiraled out of control, and chaos had ensued. Adulterers, murderers, cheats, and wicked greed-filled souls were everywhere, filled with intentions of corruption. Half-breeds, Satan's children, possessed the lands of this hollow existence.

Evil intentions create evil actions, and those actions become examples for all who watch.

The world was dying, and people caused nothing but destruction, pain, and suffering for their kin. Desperation and emptiness were all that was known, and the righteous suffered unfathomable eradication by men. The only thing that could be done would be to purify and cleanse the lands of the impure and wicked, with a flood so mighty it would wash away the tears of the Earth.

The Earth cried and cried as she bled with despair and hopelessness.

After Eve had slipped away from the tense grasp of reality, her soul was thrown into an entirely different realm, one that didn't include baby angels and delicate harps, but instead a man named Noah. Now she was Naamah, but Eve was not lost to her.

After passing through the luminescent veil between life and death, she was thrown back into the reality of this now tainted dimension. When she emerged, however, she was no longer the same person she had been when she had left; she was changed entirely. She believed whatever had happened to her was her Father's will, and she feared that by her sin, she had been punished with the curse of immortality.

Though the darkness was not permanent, the fear was still present. She dared to wonder if she had permanently destroyed her connection with the Almighty God by her wrongdoings. Had she been cast away and banished from entrance into Heaven? It would not be until many years later that she would come to realize that her "life" was far from over.

It was darkness that filled the room, not light. It was before sunrise, and thus time to rise. The straw mat she lay on was far from pleasant, leaving her with a sore back and aching joints. When she got up, she stretched her limbs and proceeded to brush out her long dark hair. The task was meticulously long, but it gave her time to reflect and think about what she would do that day.

She left the tent and made her way down to the stream, where several women were already up collecting water. Sitting at the bank, she gazed at her reflection in the water. Though she was young, her face showed signs of aging, a thought that brought nothing but acknowledgement.

Wrinkles creased her forehead and lines adorned her mouth and eyes. The russet brown orbs gleamed up at her from the gently glowing water, mistrusting and distant. Life had hardened her and made her once pure heart cold. Her fears consumed her, like they had done so very long ago in the Garden. She splashed the cool liquid over her face and washed off the impurities of the previous day. It was time to start again.

Her husband Noah was a righteous man, with a passion for God so unlike that of the other people of this land. He was a holy man, not without flaws, but divine all the same. He was the only one who could comprehend the power of Yahweh, and the only one who held the key to the right door. His reverent fear of God blessed him with the ability to discover faith's secrets: that one could be saved from sin, and that God is ever faithful to his promises.

Noah had not always been like this, however, of that she was certain. Naamah often wondered if she was sent to this time just for the purpose of meeting Noah. Perhaps God wanted him to change her and show her how wrong she was. Or, perhaps as a punishment, He forced her to see the corruption of this time, to strike guilt and fear into her heart. Everywhere she looked she could see the remnants of her mistake, and the long endless suffering that transpired.

It is not the world that is bad, but the people that give her a bad name.

She saw it in the eyes of her great-grandchildren as they turned against one another, not remembering the purity in which they could have existed. She saw it in the way the men looked at women, with hunger and lust in their eyes.

She saw it when women tried to look beautiful using worldly means. She saw it in the children also, as they fought and hurt each other, following the despicable examples set for them. As the men turned to stone and the women wept behind their cloaks, and as children vandalized and were disowned, the world grew darker and darker.

Darkness is a force, just as light is a force, but neither can exist without the other.

She remembered the single instance in which she discovered Noah's vulnerability, the only weakness she had ever seen in him. He seemed too perfect to surrender to something so simple and typical, but as she watched him lying flat on the ground with the distinct aroma of alcohol around him, she realized he was only human too.

No matter how perfect a person may seem, everyone has something imperfect about them.

Every person has flaws and hurts and makes mistakes, except Noah...or so she had thought. The little voice in her head constantly nagged her, saying how wonderful and perfect and *righteous* of a man he was. Oh, how God must have loved him so. In all of the madness of the world, there was one white lamb to be found in the midst of the hungry wolves. She could not really grasp the reality that the holiest man she had ever known could have such an *ordinary* vice.

They say every person either has a vice, a dark secret, or an unfathomable fault.

She was very disconcerted. In a way, she had always seen Noah as someone greater, perhaps a higher being come to save others with his *wise words* and good morals. He always made it seem as if he understood far greater matters than she, which he probably did; yet now she couldn't imagine him being deserving of knowing anything more than anyone else.

For all the time that she had known him, she had truly believed that Noah was favoured highly because he was undeniably perfect. Who was she to assess God's judgement, after all? But now, things had changed, and she was no longer unaware of the truths lying right before her.

We often either see the best or the worst in people. We never just see people.

She remembered a time where things were simpler, before she had come to know people in all of their imperfections. She had been tethered to hope by a thin rope. When the rope snapped, it destroyed any ounce of compassion and joy she had. Marrying Noah was what helped her remain grounded and carry on with an existence that would otherwise have felt entirely pointless. Noah was the person who taught her that despite the fires burning around you, trying to catch you, love could still be present.

She had lived for many decades with peace, until now. The only support she had, the hand holding her and preventing her from plummeting down the slippery slope of life, had let go. She was falling quickly, down and deep into the abyss of the canyon of doubts, secrets, and lies.

Naamah was angry, furious because she could not imagine that she had once felt love for this man. How could God resent her so, to put her on an empty Earth where happiness and love could never exist?

Why would He bring Noah into her life? To show her that she was not as good as His favoured child? She had come before all other women, and birthed a civilization of true horror and pain. Now, she was forced to carry this guilt on her shoulders for all of eternity, and where was He? Had He forsaken her so soon?

She was no longer able to see the merciful, thoughtful, ever-forgiving Father that claimed to love all. There would no longer be hope. She was Eve, and she helped ruin this Earth when she gave up and surrendered to her own fears and flaws.

We are all broken people, but we choose if we allow God to put the broken pieces back together again, or not.

She felt full of vengeance and hate, so she left the place where she grew up, the stone city so near the Garden that was the beginning of her inexplicable story. She fled to the mountains, escaping the chaos yet taking her profound pain with her. She travelled by foot, running, and never stopping to take in the reality of the information bombarding her thoughts. To the mountains she went, seeking to be up high, far from the ground where from dust monsters, not people, were born.

Once reaching a particular point, hidden from all sides by greenery, she stopped. With a burning, overwhelming sense of frustration and emotion, she cried out to the skies, "Father, why did you leave me alone?"

And in that split second everything seemed to fall apart. The years spent trying to figure out why she had been reborn without any sense of direction, without knowing what to think of herself and of her mistakes, became scarily more vivid. She was at a loss for what to do, but wasn't quite certain that she wanted any answers at all.

> *Sometimes we just don't know anymore, and that truth can be more frightening than anything else that could ever happen to us.*

She wept and wept, for what felt like hours on end. The pain and fear sucked away all the energy she possessed, and she felt herself falling deeper and deeper still. The haziness and disconnection from reality she had felt for the past few decades were vaporized, and her current situation was now more real than ever before.

She had felt *so alone* for so long that she often wrestled with the idea that perhaps this life was all just a dream, a distorted illusion. She had been so disconnected and detached from people and the situations going on around her because she was lost in her own world of doubts and fears.

Now, more than ever, she could recall events that played a significant role in shaping the person she was today. Memories of her childhood burned sharply through her mind, and all she could do was experience the terrors *all over again*.

> *Isn't it funny how a single moment can bring our whole world crashing down?*

When she first became alive as Eve, she was already a woman, and had the mind of an adult. When she died...she came into this world as a lost child, one with neither family nor friend. *Oh, what an anomaly it is, to see with adult's eyes from a child's perspective.* It was but a few days after she became aware of being reborn, in the form of a child, that she was noticed by a small cluster of women, both young and old, by a riverbank.

She remembered it more clearly than any other event. She recalled sitting by the stream and watching as the women filled jugs with water. She was so very thirsty, and wished to drink some of the water, but the stream was deep and moved quickly. She was afraid that if her small form reached into the water she would be pulled in and drowned instantly by the dark, threatening flow.

> *Deep waters lead to lost, hidden treasures and mysteries unfathomable to humankind; we know so little.*

Her mind was childlike then, despite containing a complete recollection of her life as Eve; those memories felt distant and faded in comparison to the reality of the present. It was almost as if she was looking at a picture that, over time, had grown faint and blurry.

From a distance, she watched the ladies, the women who worked so hard and endured so much. It was then that she looked into *her* eyes. The eyes filled with love and compassion, deep honey-coloured eyes that held no pity, only hope. The young maiden came to her and took her as her own, naming her Naamah. It meant delightful, and Naamah was her joy.

The woman taught her many things. She showed Naamah how to prepare meals and make practical clothing. She taught her how to heal others and how to really *sincerely* pray. She was holy, and she taught young Naamah about the beauty of God the Father, and despite the child's uneasiness, the young woman accepted the girl and was patient.

Naamah began to love her Father again, because she could really see Him in *her*. The grace and elegance she witnessed, the purity and willingness to help others even when they hurt you, taught her to be better. And she grew up, she lived a peaceful life and became a fine, young woman, just like her wonderful mother.

Good or bad past experiences can influence the people we are, but in the end, it is only about one thing: who we fight to become.

Anyone who knew what her mother was like took advantage of her good nature. She was cast away and treated poorly, and mocked for her innocence and virginity, despite it being a virtue. She never let it bother her, though; or at least, she never showed it.

She never hurt anyone back, and was the striking image of an angel clothed in simple, modest robes. Until they tainted the white purity, and dark, heavy splotches of red began to appear everywhere. They did more than take her life. They took her innocence, and that was the greatest crime of all.

Naamah remembered how she found the body, abandoned and contaminated with the dirt of the underground. After that, she never spoke of holiness or innocence again. Instead, she buried her goodness and allowed her soul to be corrupted by evil once more.

The two had been making their way back home through the city after returning from gathering in the woods. As on any other day, their long cloaks and veils covered their faces and obscured their true persons.

It was a biweekly ritual. To protect themselves from the predators of the land, they would hide under the safety of the shadows. And when all were asleep in the darkness of the night, the tiny lamp in their home was lit, and they lived their lives in solitude.

Alas, one could not survive solely in the night, scavenging for food and to obtain the essential living necessities. Thus, once every fortnight, the two would venture out in the early mornings to gather herbs for medicine or berries and nuts for food, and to purchase any goods they needed from the dirty, observant vendors. When dusk came they retrieved water, and just before dawn they checked their hunting traps. Throughout the night, they guarded the tiny perimeter of their tiny stone house. They worshipped through prayer and song, and thanked God for the protection He granted them each and every day.

That day, as they briskly headed to their destination, Naamah's mother was alert and cautious. As always, she kept a careful eye on every person they passed, fearing they would lay hands on her young daughter. She became very distraught and terrified upon realizing she and Naamah was being closely followed. The crowded city was difficult to get around, yet filled with numerous alleys and hidden pathways. Surely there would be an escape.

Naamah recognized the look in her mother's eye and the sudden change in her posture, stiff and ready for an attack. The two tried to lose their tailgaters by hurrying through narrow passageways and hidden corridors. Around every corner were hawk-like eyes and crooked smiles. Death awaited them shortly. It was the flip of a golden coin that signaled which of the two would be the target for the day. It was not Naamah.

The monsters drove them out of the crowded areas of the city and into the underground vaults where items were stored for trade. It was dark in the underground, and water dripped from the ceilings, adding to the ever-growing eerie feeling they were experiencing. It was there that Naamah was forced to say goodbye, as her mother forcibly ushered her through a trapdoor that led to the outside world. Her mother's voice was firm and unbreaking as she told her to be brave and never forget the beauty of love.

Naamah remembered the wooden door slamming shut hard against the frame, and the dust that arose from the earth around it. Out in the world, she was alone.

Having no place else to go, she ran to her home, where she hoped her mother would soon return. In the silence she waited, huddled by the light of the tiny lamp, praying and hoping for a sudden change of events. Despite the flame burning, she felt the suffocating grasp of darkness come over her again, and she remembered when she was Eve.

In the swirling haze of thoughts and murmur of her pleas, she came to realize many things. Her mother was intelligent for finding a home on the outskirts of the city, as it allowed for time to run should any attack come. She was brave for having left her parents at a young age, when she realized they were evil and uncaring. And her mother had been kind, for taking Naamah in when she was already broken herself.

Hours went by, and Naamah held her breath for minutes at a time. She was shivering, but sought out no blanket for comfort nor heat. As streaks of hazy orange began to paint the skies beyond the window, Naamah feared it was too late.

Before the city awoke, she grabbed her cloak and made her way to the vaults below. Upon arriving at the place where she had seen her mother last, her terror only increased tenfold. Streaks of red adorned the floors and walls around her. Treading through the tunnel-like space, she followed a path that would lead her to nothing good.

At the end of the road, one often finds a suitable destination, or a lesson that teaches about life. Difficult journeys are supposed to lead to happy endings, or a place of peace where one can finish their story with the satisfaction and affirmation that they have completed something great. Naamah found no such thing. An affirmation, perhaps, but only of her worst fears.

Her mother's corpse was cast away at the end of the tunnel. There had been no attempt made to hide it, as there was no conviction for crimes here. Naamah knelt brokenly next to the corpse, grasping the hand of the woman who gave her everything. The men that caught her used her, destroyed her, and then killed her, for she was nothing to them. In this world of mayhem, there was no mercy, even for people who did nothing but good.

She had wanted to bury her mother next to their home, but she was forced to leave when the workers arrived at the vaults and began yelling at her for trespassing. She ran, and left her mother behind in the vaults, and never returned below the Earth. Her mother, however, would lie there until she faded to dust, for not a soul would care enough to take her above, out of the belly of the beast.

Naamah had promised herself then that if she ever heard anything from God again, it would be a simple statement to condemn her for all her wrongdoings. *My child, you have a heart of gold, but your mind can be a cold, dark place.* And that would destroy every hope that maybe, just maybe, her life wasn't all just a nightmarish hell. But hope is a curious thing. It doesn't vanish overnight—it takes something truly awful to destroy it forever. So, she hoped that she was far from broken.

She grew up in isolation, just as she had before she had her mother. When she was older, things began to change, as new opportunities were introduced. When she met Noah, she was a young adult, working several jobs to afford a living.

Noah was in awe of her beauty and recognized the good in her, being a man of God. They began to speak frequently, and enjoyed each other's company. Naamah felt at ease for the first time in nearly a decade, and she was amazed that she had found a soul who cared for things other than self-satisfaction.

What Naamah hadn't expected was for Noah to ask her to be his wife. She surprised herself even more when she said yes. In the years that followed they had several children, and lived the most decent lives one could have in a city like theirs. She was happy for a while, having been freed from the ever-grasping solitude. But in time, her children grew up, as all children do, and left her for their own families. Her husband became preoccupied with fulfilling his God's word, that she would have no part in, and she was all alone again. It was in the silence that the doubts and fears crept up again, and she became aware of the imperfections in her life, starting with Noah.

And on the mountain, she lay; far above the vaults, her old home, and the partying voices of the citizens. Alone once more.

It came to her in a sudden dream of light. She heard the distant voice of an angel calling her name. "Naamah," it whispered, "it is time now to return, for a terrible storm is coming. Leave now, Naamah, a storm is coming. Leave now, and you shall be saved."

The voice was certain and powerful, leaving no room for debate. She did not miss the underlying sense of urgency it held, and the way it made her want to listen. She awoke with a start and found herself in the same place where she had fallen asleep, on the grand mountain. She gathered herself together and scampered down the slope, not pausing to notice the lack of bird cries in the air.

When she approached the dead silence of her modest home, she was hit with a sudden epiphany. The *ark*—the *end*. She raced and thrashed through vendor's tents and stone buildings, pushing past people and yelling useless apologies behind her back.

She arrived at the site devoid of the usual crowds and could only stare in awe at the astronomical size of the vessel before her. It had taken decades to construct, and she had seen it on many occasions, but on this day it seemed more real than ever. Not a single person was around other than Noah, almost as if they were purposely disregarding the masterpiece.

Noah had never told anyone the real reason for needing to build the ship; he only implied that it was the direct will of God. That was the sole reason Naamah never questioned his decision to begin the impossible and rather deranged quest to build the colossal invention.

Questions don't always yield great answers, but they reveal what is on one's mind, and often that is in itself an answer that brings the greatest realizations of self.

She approached Noah with great hesitation, but when he turned to her his eyes lit up with relief and haste.

"Naamah, hurry, there is not much time left!" he roared.

She rushed over to him, and in her fear she forgot all of her previous anger and embraced him. He ushered her into the ark and bolted the entrance shut, leaving them with no way out. It was then that she became aware of the presence of her sons and their wives, as well as *hundreds and hundreds* of animals.

She could not comprehend the meaning of this rather absurd assembly, until she realized that for each animal, there was only a male and a female. In that very second everything became clear... This was the complete annihilation of mankind.

This was it. God had come to purge the world of all the sin and evil. He was starting over, so that the new generation might have a chance at survival. The corruption was too great, as the women of Earth had borne children with demons and produced Nephilim. Those monstrosities, and the undeniable curses placed on the Earth, were too harsh and too cruel. She could fathom it no longer.

As Naamah gazed out a window at the highest point on the ship, she stood in a stupor. Water began to flood the world and purge the hills from the blood of the wicked. The cries of every demon and living thing was heard that day, but never again. There was no resurrection for the truly dead.

Some believe in the "greater good" while others really just do what's best.

Many days passed, and Naamah wondered if they would ever see land again. The water rose and rose higher, and the ship creaked and groaned under the constant pressure. The families were afraid and stayed close together, the screeches and cries of the animals the only conversation.

They prayed, and did their best to remain warm in the wet, muddy interior of this rather unsinkable ship. Made almost entirely of wood, yet powerful enough to withstand a storm such as this, Noah did not build this ship without the help of God.

After yet another seven consecutive days, they began to sing and dance to make the rain go away. Their cries were not yet answered, but in that moment they were sure that God would not forget them. They hoped that this chaos would soon come to an end, but the new world was far from ready for them, so they waited on.

Naamah often wondered if she should have died with the world. She was no better than any other person; she was perhaps worse than them all. She believed that she did not deserve God's mercy, regardless of whether He intended it for her, or to pacify Noah. Yet here she was, in the protection of the very creation of God, waiting to be brought safely home.

After forty days and forty nights, the wait was over, and a dove came with an olive leaf clutched in its beak, a clear sign that land had been found. For the following many years of her life, Naamah contemplated the importance of mercy, and how important it was when it came to new beginnings.

God did not forget her. Instead He waited until the perfect opportunity to show her the right path, and brought her home. Perhaps she was a sinner, yes, but she was offered rescue by the most High King. And perhaps, that was enough to say that she may still have a chance.

We are all deserving of second chances, but beyond that, nobody ever really knows.

CHAPTER THREE:
A SNAKE BITE FOR RA

Perhaps it was unreasonable of her to expect that things could have taken a turn for the better. Nonetheless, she remained optimistic. Building the new world was no easy task, and after decades of hard work cultivating the land and taking care of her grandchildren, Naamah let go and fell into death's waiting arms. She passed away surrounded by loved ones and with her frail, old, tired bones. When she awoke again, however, a lot of time had passed.

*And back again she was in a world she didn't know; a
world of poisoners, liars, and gold.*

The Nile River was a creation as majestic as a gold tomb holding the secret treasures of the dead. It both provided for the land by allowing survival, and destroyed it by its mighty floods. The gift of life and death; both a blessing and a curse. Like everything else, it held promises of both good and evil. Undoubtedly, it was a force of its own.

There is a force inside of us that calls us to be bold, a force that compels us to say what was never told.

The day was brighter than any she had ever seen before. Sunlight shimmered upon the water as a kind gift of warmth from Ra. She gazed upon the ancient river, which armies had once travelled across to battle enemies for the sake of power and destiny.

The same water had enabled Alexander the Great to conquer this land many decades ago. He had ruled nations with an iron fist and the heart of a cobra, the king. Now, as the descendent of the first of the Macedonian Greeks to conquer Egypt, she would ensure that the Ptolemy dynasty would remain unconquered, by any possible means.

Iron fist or gentle hand; both can cause destruction if you let them have your land.

She glanced down at the orb resting in her elegant hands. The gold jewelry contrasted wickedly with the mysterious allure of the purple smoke rising inside the glass. Her long, sharp nails trailed over the surface as she prepared to watch the secrets unfold. Bringing the orb up to her lips, she whispered, "Show me what I wish to know."

Images formed from the smoke, rising and falling and twisting until they molded, as if from clay, into shapes. She saw others like her, others that *were* her. She saw a woman standing before crowds of millions, before she faded and was replaced by a queen on her throne. At first, Cleopatra thought the queen must represent herself, but this queen wore a different crown. As this thought formed, the image split into two, and there were suddenly two queens back-to-back. One, a pharaoh woman, and the other a noblewoman. Parallels, she realized. Two sides of the same coin. They too faded, before the smoke formed an odd winged vehicle that seemed to soar through the air.

Cleopatra placed the orb in its obsidian holder and moved towards the large window overlooking the city. She pondered what she had witnessed, and allowed the presence of Spirit to give her insights. *Parallels.* It seemed that she had learned a very significant secret about her existence: time did not matter. She was only one of infinite realities, perhaps realities existing simultaneously. There was no strict timeline, and with every life, she would experience a journey far different than the previous ones.

But alas, as she went back and forth through time, not all of her experiences would give her insights and wisdom. After all, with every new life, the memories became hazy and the details faded. She figured this was only fair; perhaps knowing too much of what the future held could be dangerous, even if you already experienced it. The only thing she would be able to truly carry with her would be the lessons she learned.

The glorious smell of lavish perfumes filled every inch of the carpet she was securely wrapped in. It was her destiny to appeal to the Roman Empire and create an allegiance to benefit the Egyptian Empire. Her ships deftly swept into the magnificent harbour of Rome, and the young woman soon found herself within the private quarters of Julius Caesar, as a complete packaged delivery.

She heard the exchange between men in the room and soon enough, the carpet was unrolled. She emerged in all her glory, spreading her vivacious presence across the room. She gazed into the amused eyes of the man in front of her, her own eyes filled with pride.

*The unexpected often occurs at the oddest of moments and
in the strangest of places.*

She was far from bothered by the fact that Caesar was not capti-
vated by her beauty; he, of course, had an endless parade of women
at his disposal. But of course, she would be different, because she
had brilliant strategies and many other means of bribery.

Intelligence is a truly great beauty in itself.

"Cleopatra the Seventh Philopator, pharaoh of Egypt and
descendant of Alexander the Great. It is a *pleasure* to meet your
acquaintance." His voice held an edge of sarcasm, yet she was
not troubled.

"And I you," the young woman replied while giving a dramatic
bow. "I heard about your troubles with Pompey, but it seems you
just managed to end that rather touching struggle. A pity really,
that I couldn't have participated. I would have been a rather *prom-
ising* asset. Perhaps in the future."

It was imperative that she persuaded him of her power, otherwise he would never consider doing business with her. But after
her words, his piercing laugh rang out in the empty room. "That,
I have no doubt of," he replied, with humour evident in his voice.

"Do you question my power, with your mockery so evident on
your tongue? Do you really want to question my capabilities when
you are drowning in your very own debt?" she hissed.

He immediately sobered. "My dear woman, you do not know
the very half of it. And that is why I wish to make an allegiance
with you."

"Very good," she seethed. "It seems the mighty ruler is still
capable of making decent decisions. But first, I need a favour."

"And how may I be of assistance?"

"I have a certain younger brother I wish to bring an end to, as he holds much of the power I desire, if I am to serve Egypt well. Surely you of all people understand that, Julius?"

"I am very aware that Ptolemy the Thirteenth has betrayed you; you may rest assured that my armies will defeat him. I ask only that you allow me to keep warships on the Nile, as my suspicions of Pompey's associates are still present. The war is not yet over, not until his every last descendent is finished."

"Your will is my will."

"Then I will accompany you to Alexandria, my queen. Where we will both finally get what we have always, *always* wanted."

Is it love, or is it lust? Is it power, or is it unjust?

They ruled together, they destroyed together, and they took back what was always theirs. She learned about family and how it was a poison, always causing conflict, and she realized that only she could save herself.

They had *betrayed* her, trying to take power for themselves, and had cast her away. Her *brother* and his *guardians*. Blood is thick, but water flows so much more easily. But now, now their blood would flow quickly and drown in the great depths of the Nile.

Just like you choose friends, you choose family.

She got what she wanted. When the deal was fulfilled, Caesar left and returned to Rome to do what he was destined to do: rule. She named his son Ptolemy Caesar, who was called Caesarian in honor of the powerful alliance that forever altered the course of history.

Ruling alongside her second brother, Ptolemy the Fourteenth, she established control and was celebrated as an idol. Of course, she occasionally had to visit Rome, as she could never be left out of the triumphant parades and festivities taking place to honour Caesar. She reveled in the humiliation and terror of their defeated enemies as they were paraded through the streets.

She would later recall seeing a young girl amongst a crowd of enemies, and would be elated when she recognized her as Arsinoe, her *sister*. Families are torn apart in tragedy, sometimes broken beyond repair, and other times they can be restored.

But she was not so forgiving. A magnificent gold-plated statue built in her honour was placed in the Temple of Venus Genetrix. Of course, it should have been adorned in gems.

> *The definition of beauty is so limited, as it is different in every place.*

When word of Caesar's assassination reached her, she was not surprised, nor stricken. She immediately returned to Alexandria, where she made the decision to annihilate her co-ruler, or *brother*, as they say. All it took was some *poison*.

Caesarian would now be her co-reagent, until someone more formidable could take that place. She did have a particular person in mind, someone that would be far too easy to tempt. Caesar's successor, Marcus Antonius, who went by Mark Antony, was a true leader. Word came that he desired her aid in his conquest to overthrow the Persian Empire; he needed financial and military help. How could she deny the request?

> *Broken people either give up or give in to the madness that turns them into monsters.*

When they met in Tarsus, she feigned the need for a *strong* Roman leader to protect her, now that Caesar was gone. She was an exceptional actress and had the mind of a philosopher. She mesmerized him with knowledge and wisdom, her charm coming not from her beauty but from her intellect.

He was undeniably naïve, and was easily dominated in the battle of desire. His plans were sacrificed in pursuit of the *love of his life*, which was exactly what she had foreseen. She took him to Alexandria, where the fun could really begin.

Snakes are vicious and vile, but their cunning always gets them what they want.

Mark ruled firmly and unyieldingly, keeping his promise to stand by her side. He did what Caesar could never do: be her equal. And as all stories go, a common enemy emerged. Battles ensued, causing inevitable sacrifices and a battle of wills. Julius's adopted son, Octavian, struck a treaty with the insurance being that Mark would marry his sister, Octavia.

In order to protect their power this contract was fulfilled. In addition, the assassination of Arsinoe ensured that Cleopatra's enemies would never use her to overthrow the throne. Soon enough, things began to fall apart, as they always seem to. Octavian and Mark refused to work together, and war was unavoidable, and crucial.

War is tragic, but changes the course of history forever.

She never believed that she would fall like this. In a deluded sense, she truly believed she was a goddess amongst gods, invincible. The battle brought bloodshed and terror to all, especially the losing side. And they were the losing side. She did her best to prevent the *foreseen prophecy* and save her men by taking her ships out of the fatal battle. She was not prepared for the consequences that began to unfold as a result of her mistake.

He lost everything because of her. Mark Antony, her lover and partner, lost *everything.* How he managed to escape when no one else was left, she would never know. But on her ship, together for days, she still could not relent and accept her mistake.

To be honest, as time passed on, she could not say that she was even remotely sorry. There was no emotion of love in her; there never really had been. It was always about power. The power that breathed loudly, and gave her the greatest pleasure and satisfaction in the world.

The knowledge that she could have everything under her control, everything in her power to change, was invigorating. She was not a good person; she never could be when she was so addicted to control. But she was not ready to lose control, at least not when she still had a chance.

Why do you hold on to the things you cannot control? Let go of what does not serve you.

Perhaps that is the reason she felt reawakened when Octavius' letter unveiled a plot that would once again sway the power into her open arms. He promised that if she killed Mark Antony, they would be able to work out an agreement. Of course Cleopatra couldn't refuse; the only problem was her ability to complete such a nefarious task. It had nothing to do with the relationship, more so with her limited resources and opportunities.

Something awakened within her then, crawling from under the flesh. It gave her clarity and insight. The fiendish plot could be completed with something as simple as paper and ink. After all, words have power, maybe even the most power of all the weapons in the world.

She would hit him where it would hurt most, the heart. No dagger, sword, nor arrow; he would be the end of himself. She carefully scrawled out a letter depicting her great sorrows and grief at the fall of their reign together in Egypt, and her tragic final solution of ending her own life. If he loved her as he said he did, the despair would finish him off quickly.

There is nothing more easily swayed than the heart, and grief is the downside of love.

She found him later in their private quarters, fallen upon his sword. The life was still in his eyes, but fading quickly. When he recognized her, she understood the betrayal he felt before he showed it, and the sorrow and disappointment.

He sputtered out an apology, what for, she knew not, and then begged her to make peace with Octavian. Perhaps he really did care for her until the end, but now he was gone.

Nothing hurts more than being stabbed in the back by the people you thought would always love you.

She realized later that she was used. She was used to bring an end to herself, just like she made Mark be the bringer of his own death. She would never be accepted into society again; her time as a ruler was over. If she was not to be paraded through the cities in Octavian's victory march, then she would do well to end it all quickly now, as the other outcome would be far worse.

We often question our choices after we experience the repercussions of them.

Her last hope was to protect Caesarion, as he was the heir to the throne. She sent him and his protectors far away, willing that fate proved to be on her side. She planned to die as a phoenix would, from fire into ashes, in the hope of being reborn. In her mausoleum, where her treasures laid, she would die as her riches disappeared from the world, for no one to ever find.

But as the fire rose around her in the room, she heard footsteps approaching, and loud voices roared over the sound of crackling flames. As the smoke filled her lungs, she felt hands grab her and pull her away. Her eyes rolled back into her head and she fell limp.

Flames provide warmth and light, but also death, destruction, and despair.

When she awoke again, she found herself in a cold, unlit cell. Frustration and an undeniable anger fueled her to curse viciously at the thought of Romans thwarting her plans. Octavian believed he had won and wished to humiliate her, leaving her without the ability to die honourably. The last thing she wished to do was be executed in front of thousands, where they would mock her defeat and laugh at her foolishness.

What would we do to avoid humiliation and discomfort?

Sitting in the prison cell, her deepest fears resurfaced for the first time in decades. She had become prideful and arrogant in pursuit of finding security in luxury and power. And now, she understood, she would be reduced to nothing once more. From the corner of her eye, she saw an asp emerge from a basket of figs.

Fate is a curious thing, as it turns our lives into fantastical stories.

A snake. How fitting, that it would be her demise. She stared into its alluring emerald eyes and understood the message being sent. "*By the snake's power you once died, and by the snake's intelligence you will fall again.*"

The gentle hissing noise increased in volume and gave off an aura of persuasion, as if attempting to get her to accept her fate. She knew it was useless to attempt to fight what was meant to be.

She had no power against the higher beings. To them she was nothing, and now they would force her to become aware of her weakness. The asp encircled her wrist and slithered up to her arm to rest on her shoulder.

She was Cleopatra the Seventh, Philopator. She was not a pharaoh, nor a ruler, nor a queen. She was simply a person, no different than any other, powerless.

As the sharp-tipped fangs penetrated her chest and the venom entered her body, she could only fathom how she wasted so much time hiding from who she truly was, and this time she was so, *so* sorry.

Remember who you really are, before you become someone you will later learn to hate.

CHAPTER FOUR:

FORGIVENESS IN DEATH

Twill not be long 'till the end of days, they will say. Behold, the coming of the good Lord and the end to all our sorrows and woes. Indeed, t'is right. Woes and sorrows, grief and famine, poverty and chaos on every dark corner of this world.

Rats and such pestilence are not even lowly enough to be comfortable on this barren place. 'Tis not long 'till the end of war, and maybe then we shall be happy again, the people say. Such vile and utterly vicious behaviour can only last so long, after all. Perhaps, until the enemies grow tired and surrender, we should play a bit of a game. Hiding and seeking for the place that was once ours. We shan't find it, for it is no more.

One day we'll be lost, far more than we already are. 'Tis almost the end of dawn, and then we can finally be gone. The noise never stops, and goes on through day and night. 'Tis only lament and forgotten hope that we will one day be liberated.

There is only insanity here, as the men and women grow hungry and more hungry as time fades and fades away. Have we been forgotten in this time of worldly crisis? We were intended to be a neutral ground, a place without hostility. Truces can be made and people can promise, yet truces are still broken and people lie harshly.

We are the oppressed, the neglected, the starved. It seems our roots go back only so far. Our cities were taken, destroyed and never to be found. Our people bruised and battered, killed and gone. We live in this place, for we cannot ever escape. We hope only for a reason that others may benefit from our situation. We have little hope for heroes, as we always fought alone. We are the Dutch, and the Netherlands has been lost.

They hear whispers in the night, whispers of broken promises and endless lies.

The black ink struck against the worn paper as she wrote, allowing her innumerable thoughts to come to life. She spoke of her country, her fellow people, and the wars that befouled the land. Marguerite Janssen was the name her father gave her when she was adopted in the year 1914, the beginning of the First World War. He had known that time well, served in the war and fought with much pride. Their family honored him, and remembered his sacrifices with doubtless gratitude. He was a brave man, and had even won many great war trophies. The only thing her family won back was his body after he was killed in action.

Now, decades later, she can think only of her mother, and how she likely felt then how Marguerite felt now. The pain and grief at the thought of knowing that your dear husband is far from home, likely living in a cold and grimy trench with little hope for a future, is the heart-wrenching experience they currently shared.

Her husband, a well-known author, was living with the smell of rotting flesh and the sound of raining bomb shells over his head. The idea of returning home to his wonderful family was the only thing keeping him from giving up. Her children, Lotte and Daan, barely more than seven years of age, were twins who had never known any fear besides that of the monsters under their beds.

Now, however, they would be forced to witness terrors that would not just be their imagination, if she didn't protect them.

It's funny how after realizing our terrible mistakes, our persona is often changed forever.

After the pharaoh had passed, she was thrown into a world that was beyond dissimilar from her own. Modern Europe during a time of war was terrifying enough for people acquainted with the era, but for someone who had lived millennia ago, it was beyond inconceivable.

She found herself in an orphanage, at a time where children were treated harshly. With the memories of being a great ruler who was waited on by everyone hand and foot, it was a truly humbling experience. This time made her recall her life as Naamah, where things were simpler, despite the chaos around her.

Sometimes we just need a reminder to be thankful for everything that we have; but then again, some people just need a slap in the face.

They rationed what they could, of course, and went many days without any meat or dairy. This frustrated her, as growing children needed proper nourishment. They broke bread made from the toughest of grains and put their greatest efforts in growing as much produce as possible in the limited space they had in their tiny yards.

With such a small country, and much of the land being used for industrial purposes during this worldly crisis, they had little to work with. They barely had enough money to sustain themselves, much like the rest of the population, so they worked together as a community, as neighbours and family.

Unity is one of the things that make humans the most successful. Division makes us idiots.

With her completely warped ideas of family and love in her past life, she made it her mission to put all of her efforts into caring about her own kin in this life. She recognized the loveliness and satisfaction that came from doing good things for other people, and felt better than she ever did when she had only power.

There are more important things in life than money and power, like love, kindness and hope.

She recalled times when she was a small girl, very young and confused about the world around her; she had seen far too many atrocious things happening. Her mother had been a volunteer nurse in one of the hospitals, the *Reinier de Graaf Gasthuis Ziekenhuis* in the city of Delft.

She remembered asking her mother why she was never allowed to go with her to watch her help the soldiers. Her mother had kneeled down, and taking her daughter's hands in hers, strictly commanded, "Marguerite, you will never go to the Ziekenhuis, unless you wish to never be the same again."

Her mother's kind face had been etched with worry, and she had looked into her daughter's eyes and made her promise to never go to the hospital. Marguerite was disappointed at first, because she wanted to be like her brave mother and help others, but eventually relented and promised her mother she would stay away.

As all children do in time, she forgot. Weeks went by, and soon enough no memory of the conversation with her mother remained in her mind. Then, one day, she was walking home from school with her friends Ivonne and Oneida, when she saw a little boy playing with an army knife and a hand grenade.

Memories, memories, memories; that's all anything really is in the end.

When she had edged closer to where he sat, she was able to recognize him as Lukas, the six-year-old son of Ellen and Hans van Dijk—and the town's "nutcase" as the other children said. Everyone knew there was something strange about the boy; he always seemed to stare out into space, and rarely spoke. He was a very quiet boy and many other children made fun of him, as they did not understand the delicate matters hiding behind the family's cheerful facade.

Lukas' father had been one of the first to enlist in the war. Not a month later, he had returned without half of his face, and many tragic memories.

It was common knowledge to the neighbors that Hans was severely disturbed, and often lashed out at his wife. Even Marguerite saw her in the market square on Thursday mornings, often nursing a black eye and a limp. It was no wonder that the child had found the weapons, as some days Hans thought that he was still on the battlefield, fighting to return to his family.

Memories of the past plague us, and the future seems so far away.

Marguerite had watched, frozen in terror, as the boy fidgeted with the "toys" across the street. She had been trapped in a flash-back, recalling when her mother had once warned her to be cautious of foreign items, because they could hurt others.

Perhaps not knowing is saving yourself from fear; however, ignorance is a bliss that we often get used to.

Ivonne snapped her out of the stupor when she marched forward and knelt ten feet in front of Lukas. She spoke to him kindly, but not without an edge of fear in her voice. "Lukas, look at me. Those are weapons. They are dangerous, and you could get hurt very badly if you don't leave them be."

Lukas was paying attention now, but he seemed disturbed. "No. My papa gave me these souvenirs from the war. They're mine."

"I know they are, but if you continue to play with them then your mama will be very upset."

"Why?"

Ivonne had glanced back at Marguerite and Oneida, with a pleading look that said, help, please.

Marguerite had stepped forward and approached the little boy, whispering, "Lukas, if you let me borrow them, I will give you plenty of bread."

He had contemplated it, which was something the girls could all understand, as bread was scarce and everyone was hungry. Then, a look of determination had entered his eyes and he suddenly looked angry. "No. You're lying."

He had fidgeted where he sat, squirming in insubordination and ignorance. His young mind could not comprehend the implications of his innocence.

The grenade was jostled in his tiny hands, shaking as the boy's anger grew in disobedience. His fingers unconsciously slipped to the pin, and without thinking, pulled. Chaos ensued.

It's a lovely thing, chaos, isn't it? It follows you and begs for attention, until you're drowning in its love for you.

"Marguerite!!" The high-pitched voice of Ivonne had screeched in panic the moment it suspected the outcome. Marguerite had felt hands on her arms, hauling her up and away from the scene, to safety.

Ivonne had pulled her arm and the three of them ran as fast as they could before the explosion went off, and they were blasted off their feet. Marguerite's vision went black, and for a moment she believed she was dead.

Within seconds, a buzzing filled her ears and her vision gradually returned, with fuzzy images of the world around her being distorted by the blurring of her tears.

Shockwaves of pain rattled her body, and she felt bruises line her left side as she rolled onto her back. Clouds of dust rose up around her, and rubble dug into her arms as she propped herself up on her elbows. She lay there in the midst of the havoc and allowed her mind to process the insanity that was now her life.

She had gotten up from the dust-ridden cobblestone street and stumbled over to where her friends laid a couple feet away.

"Oneida, Ivonne, wake up." Her voice came out scratchy, as if she hadn't drank any water for days.

Slowly, her friends began to open their eyes and become more aware of their surroundings. Marguerite had watched as Ivonne gradually maneuvered herself into a sitting position. She could never have prepared herself for what happened next.

There's no such thing as madness, silly; insanity is simply your perception of what isn't normal, and we're all unique, aren't we?

Ivonne had fixed her gaze on a spot behind where Marguerite stood, and her confused look gradually melted into one of pure horror. Her jaw had dropped, and her mouth became a perfect circle as she let out an "oh," before fainting. Oneida was making a funny choking noise and wasn't blinking as she looked far out into the distance.

> *You really don't get it at all, do you? Don't worry, one day*
> *you'll look back at this moment and realize with a start*
> *that I was an enigma, and it had nothing to do with you.*

Marguerite had stood dumbfounded for a moment before cautiously turning around to meet with a scene out of a horror movie.

Blood was splattered everywhere, running down the streets and into the sewers. The mutilated body of the boy was scattered into irreplaceable pieces.

She had been rooted to the spot at which she stood, and had watched in alarm as the door of the van Dijk house violently slammed open and Hans emerged, holding a near-empty beer bottle. He had slogged over to where Marguerite stood, and took in the scene. He took another sip of beer before he turned over to the small girl looking up at him in fear and bellowed, "What did you do? What did *you* do?"

She didn't move. She didn't speak. She didn't react at all, even as she felt hands wrap around her throat and begin to squeeze the life out of her. The disgusting smell of alcohol had made her feel dizzy.

> *She couldn't breathe. She was dying, and no one would*
> *help her. She was really going to die.*

He had laughed at her attempts to get free. Her kicking and struggling grew stronger as the natural instinct kicked in.

"I don't want... to die." Her vision had begun to fade terribly, and it narrowed as darkness swarmed at the edges. She had begged in her mind for the nightmare to be over.

That was before she heard the crack of hard glass on a skull, and the pressure on her neck was released.

She had fallen to the floor ungracefully into a heap, and when she finally managed to catch her breath, she had seen Helen standing with the end of a bloodied beer bottle in her hand. Her breathing was ragged and tears streamed down her face but, despite the obvious grief, she remained upright.

Marguerite looked into her eyes and saw immense fear, longing, and regret. This was just one other occasion where a mother lost her child, and a drunk husband back from the war abused his wife. Her story was not much different than many. Perhaps that was what inspired Marguerite to leave her in the midst of her broken family, as she ran away to find her own.

She ran and ran until she arrived at the hospital, where she knew her mother was still working, late hours approaching the night. She had not hesitated to enter at that moment, and was greeted with the stale smell of urine and blood.

Low groans emitted from every corner, and row upon row of small cots lined the walls and center of the large hall. The sick, the wounded, the mentally ill, and the broken men, young and old, occupied every square inch of the building. Some without limbs, other without faces, and many with charred, blackened bodies.

Hope, passion, and love are what it takes for one person to give their life for another.

Ragged breathing and coughing had filled the room as frantic nurses and doctors roamed around, hoping to save yet another life. She had not been able to stop turning around and taking in the mayhem and overwhelming despair in the room.

How could any sane person allow this much tragedy and horror to be afflicted upon the fragile bodies of men? How could any being be so impure and evil to inflict this much pain and misfortune upon another?

Tears had gathered in her eyes as she stared down at her shoes, no longer willing to face the reality of the day. When she finally looked up, her mother had been gazing across the room at her with saddened features, as she too faced the reality that she could no longer protect her daughter from the inevitable truth of the truly awful world she was brought into.

Terror is the result of accepting fear's request of an invitation into your heart.

The events that had taken place so very long ago opened within her, an overwhelming turmoil of emotions and feelings that she had been too young to deal with at the time. Marguerite tried so hard to bury deep within her heart the truth of the evil of this world.

She was happy to forget it for many years, as the war ended in 1918 and she was able to grow up as a perfectly normal girl. But certain things always stopped her from moving on. She wasn't the only witness on the day that Lukas van Dijk suffered a violent death. Marguerite lived through yet another terrible occurrence when she learned that, barely two years later, Ivonne left this world in a drastic attempt to rid herself of the pain of knowing that she could not save the child. Funerals always had the same scent, she noted, of misery.

I miss you, but you're already long gone.

Oneida was only slightly better off; she was able to cope with grief, but never the memories. She did her best to bring a light into the world as the rest had been snuffed out, and remained Marguerite's friend and neighbor. There were still moments when Marguerite saw her break, as she trembled in a trance that was a result of the terrible remnants the event left in her mind.

The two women would often cry together, sharing a heavy burden that they could only carry together. Moments such as these made her realize that a part of their life was taken from them. One moment was all it took to change their lives forever, and ruin them. And now, so many years later, they would be forced to relive another terror…war.

One thing after another, and yet you're still standing.

One might've said that they could have been okay. They were resourceful, surviving with the barest minimum of supplies and food, always looking for alternatives and improvisations.

The Netherlands was a neutral party, with a signed agreement that promised they would never be attacked. The people believed this with all of their hearts, so all was well…until they learned that the Fuhrer did not believe in paper. Then all went to hell.

Don't believe everything you hear; after all, even your own ears can be mistaken.

The battle began, and they fought with such brutality and strength that they even hoped for a chance to win. Even without guns, the Dutch hid under bridges and took out armed soldiers by slitting their throats when they were otherwise occupied. They fought like animals and gave the Germans a reason to send more troops—unfortunately, that was not what they wanted.

The news spread like wildfire: they were invaded, and endured a brutal battle. Rotterdam had been bombed, so many buildings destroyed entirely, and now they were at war.

For many weeks, they brutally fought back and relentlessly shielded their families from the inevitable outcome of failure, but now, the end approached. They had lost, and they had lost badly. Very badly. They were now trapped in their own country like caged birds.

The Germans took everything from them in their brutal attempt to conquer the waterways and annihilate their enemies. Dutch citizens were slaughtered by the enemy, and then even by their own kind. Madness ensued as people became desperate for the suffering to end.

Marguerite and her family were living in Amsterdam at this time, and the capital city was never a good place to be in a time of war. Her heart went out to the children of the hunted races; the poor Jews that were being condemned for no true reason at all.

She also had her suspicions that her neighbour, Miep Gies as they call her, was helping a family stay in hiding. She said nothing, of course; the last thing she wanted to do was be responsible for ruining a family's chance of survival.

When you ask yourself whether you should help a person or not, picture yourself in their position, and imagine the emotions that come with the cry.

She noticed the signs before anyone else did, and because of that, she was *almost* prepared. Having experienced the First World War for herself, she lived with an extreme attention to her surroundings, and rationed everything as if another war would start any second.

Before the beginning of the Second Great War, she had stocked up on hundreds of cans of food and hid it all in boxes in a cellar under a rug on the pantry floor. She knew from the beginning that the following years would be difficult, and wanted to do her best to prepare for an outcome she could not control.

Knowing is security; challenges come with inexperience.

Her heart cried every day as she felt the pain and suffering of the people around her. She wanted to do nothing but help the souls of the torn victims of loss and heartbreak find peace. But she didn't. There was nothing she *could* do, at least not without putting her own family in peril.

She fell into a mundane routine of work and care. She would wake up in the chilling hours before sunrise to work at the war relief organization, return home just before eight to prepare a meager breakfast, and wake her children and begin the day of a working mother and provider.

She took on the galling task of educating her children, lying about their age to prevent them going to the mandatory public school. She never let them leave the house, unless it was with her complete supervision.

One day I'll find a reason to say I like my life, for reasons other than that I love you.

She recalled a day when she was forced to leave her home and children, to find medicine for her son, who was ill with pneumonia. Of course, it was on this day that she lost control and relapsed into the feelings of utter loneliness and despair. If she didn't keep herself distracted, she would become overwhelmed with the memories she was forced to keep. It was also then that she was reminded of the many problems she faced before, and was haunted by the trauma.

Darkness came over her, and she was cold. Shivering down to her very core, she huddled in the corner of an abandoned alleyway. The woolen cardigan wrapped around her was pressed firmly around her lithe frame. Tears streamed down her cheeks as a series of memories plagued her ancient mind. Colours swirled in the puddles of rain around her, red and menacing.

Gunshots could still be heard in the distance, but they had died down since the attack at dawn. It was nearly dusk now, and everyone was gone. Gone, gone, gone. She had never been gone, because she could never forget. She had never known an afterlife, not Heaven or the underworld run by Hades that was spoken about in Greek mythology. She had never experienced Nirvana, nor a return to a foreign place. She was simply here, forced to live with her mistakes.

Monday morning: early, cold, dull, and lonely. She began to heat up water, and soon the whistling of the kettle was apparent throughout the house. She remained unmoving, seated at the hardwood table. The small kitchen was adorned with pictures of family memories. A beautiful wedding picture was framed in wood above the dust-speckled window. It would have been quiet if not for the always present sound of planes soaring high above the fallen city. That, and the sound of trucks and tanks travelling through the streets on a never-ending quest to fight for a useless cause.

She removed the kettle and poured the hot water; they had not been able to have tea for weeks now, and she hadn't bothered to keep it in supply before the invasion. The faint sound of a gunshot rang in the background and she flinched, still not used to the sound. Another shot, another life taken, a constant reminder of the families losing loved ones.

You lost your love, and they still wish to take more of what was never really yours.

The gentle creak of the front door opening nearly caused her to have a heart attack, and she stiffened before frantically running to see who the intruder was. There she was greeted with the small form of her son Daan, standing in the shadow of a much larger, intimidating form.

Two tall, blue-eyed German soldiers stood in the doorway, armed with guns and masking faces of boredom. When they spoke, their heavy accents were obvious, but they knew the Dutch language as well, as it was so close to their own.

"Goede morgen. As you are aware, we have been issued with the task of searching all homes for any supplies and rations. The policy states that we have the right to obtain any stored products that may contribute to our important cause. Force may be used if necessary, but you seem to be an intelligent woman, so that shouldn't be a problem. Move aside please." His voice held a forceful edge that made Marguerite fearful to object. The underlying threat in his voice promised great trouble if she did not comply.

"Of course, sirs. Please come in." She smiled quite forcibly.

They entered and searched all the cabinets and drawers, finding nothing but cutlery and plates. She had prepared well for the likely possibility of an occurrence such as this. After finding nothing in the barren kitchen, one soldier went upstairs to search while the other stayed with her, Daan, and a terrified Lotte.

The little girl tugged at the hem of her mother's skirt, begging to be held, but Marguerite told her to be quiet and not cause trouble.

The soldier supervising the family looked down at the child and gruffly said, "There is nothing to fear if you have nothing to hide, little one."

Lotte immediately shied away and hid behind her mother, causing the soldier to laugh at the scene. In response, the girl peeked out from behind her mother and gave a timid, wary smile at the man.

Do you understand what I mean when I say that everyone is both good and bad, a hero and a villain, an angel and a demon?

Marguerite was immensely surprised at his attempt at kindness, so used to loud, jeering voices, cruel jokes, and mocking insults. She felt how wrong it was, for a person like him to act decently, especially with everything he had done to hurt the families of others.

Her expression must have shown some confusion, because the German chuckled and explained. "Woman, surely you must understand that not everything we do is by our own will. I have a daughter myself; her name is Lisa, and she is the only reason that I fight. I might not always like what I do, and sometimes I may question the purposes for which I do them for, but not all Germans are bad."

"But why don't you try to stop the things your leaders want you to do?" she blurted out, unable to help herself.

"Because if we do not comply, our families will be killed, just as your families are being killed in the Netherlands. I saw many of my friends die at the hands of the Dutch, and yes, you may have been defending your country, but I am protecting the people I care about when I hurt yours. It is a cruel world, and many of us are forced to things we cannot fathom."

The other soldier was making his way down the stairs and to the door, empty-handed.

"Guten Tag Frau," and then they were gone.

The extent of how far we are willing to go to save the people we love erases the limit we set for how far we will go beyond our morals.

Everything he said was true. They were all fighting a losing battle, because no matter which side won in this war, they would all lose people and things they cared about. They would all be hurt, and it was all against their will. The decisions they made would have terrible consequences, but priorities had to be made. For most of them, the priority would be family, but unfortunately, their survival would come at the price of other's.

An eye for an eye, a life for a life. And on and on it goes.

Later that day, the same soldiers visited the house next door. When they emerged, they were followed by a family: a man, a woman, and two adolescent girls. Marguerite knew immediately they were Jewish, and watched as they were forced onto prisoner trucks.

As she gazed out the window one of the girls caught her eye, and she saw the fear in the glistening orbs. The fear for her own life, and the life of her family. But within her she also saw an air of determination. She knew that somehow, someway, she would be able to impact others long after her death.

As the girl was forced to walk on, Marguerite glimpsed the necklace she wore. The following scene was forever burned in her mind: David's star being ripped from the girl's neck and thrown away, and a backhand to the face as she reached out to retrieve it. The cries of the women were like shockwaves in the silence, as they were forced to leave their refuge and likely meet their end.

Marguerite felt tear tracks on her face. She cried for the rest of the day. The sacrifice to protect her family, rather than help others, was at the price of overwhelming grief and a sense of failure.

In the end, it comes down to who and what you care about the most.

The war lasted for several more months before it came to a gradual end. The cries of joy could be heard everywhere. The Netherlands had been liberated by the Canadians, and the Germans had finally been defeated for good. Everywhere parades were held, and people expressed their gratitude by writing on rooftops and throwing celebrations.

The food sent in parcels from planes was a saving grace in the times of struggle, and the way the Dutch and Canadians fought together was inexplicably magnificent. The two countries would undoubtedly go on to be formidable allies and friends for many generations.

Marguerite was so overjoyed that her family would be able to live normal lives once more. She hoped to be reunited with her husband soon, as she had not heard from him for nearly three months. Things were finally starting to look brighter in the world.

What you don't expect hurts you the most.

Not a month later, she received a notice that her husband went missing in action nearly two months ago, right before the end of the war. She was furious at how unfair the world could be. Marguerite had just found out the day before that Oneida had been reunited with her husband Franz, and they were happily making plans to move to Switzerland.

After everything her family had been through, why was it that they had to suffer more? How was she going to explain to Daan and Lotte that their hero father was never going to return to them? She couldn't bear the reality of it all.

Heartbreak and loss. You don't really believe it until it's official; whether it be a divorce paper, breakup letter, or suicide note.

Late at night when the children were asleep, she found herself in front of the home of Miep Gies. She stared at the faded black paint on her door as she stood on her front steps, not really knowing why she was there.

Marguerite was startled when the door abruptly opened, and a pale face emerged. "I've been expecting you for quite some time now, Marguerite. Won't you please come in?" She spoke in a deep voice not devoid of empathy, nor understanding. It was not surprising that a minute later Marguerite found herself seated at the large dining room table, staring at the dull designs on the old, worn out tablecloth.

The older lady stood across the room watching her. "Would you like some tea?" she asked softly.

She listened to the familiar sound of a kettle on a stove, and she traced her rough fingers on the delicate patterns of the flowers on the cloth.

Gies spoke out with an air of certainty. "You were watching that day, weren't you? You saw them take the family?"

"Yes," she affirmed finally, lifting her gaze to look at the woman before her.

"They were a special family, you know. Especially the youngest girl." She smiled subtly as if recalling a special event in a time long ago. "I want to show you something," she voiced. She made her way over to a small, rickety table next to the sofa and opened one of the drawers.

She shifted some items around until she found what she was looking for, and in her hand emerged a red, plaid diary. Gies trudged over and handed Marguerite the book, and when she opened it she was amazed at what she saw. Countless journal entries of the events that occurred in the past few years.

Passages with such emotion and wisdom that she could not imagine belonged to a young girl. She wrote beautifully and had a way of storytelling that made it seem as if all the events she witnessed were a part of your history too. Marguerite understood everything she wrote about… the grief and desperation that came as a result of the war. But above all, she was enlightened with a very new revelation, that truly, *"what is done cannot be undone, but one can prevent it from happening again."*

The undeniable brilliance of this young girl went on to inspire many other people, and entirely changed the way everyone looked at their mistakes. This has changed people forever, in a way they could never forget.

The difference one person can make is often more powerful than the efforts of millions of people together.

But, they will have to fight to make up for their mistakes now. They must now forgive and ask for forgiveness, because in spite of everything, no matter what happened, they are all humans and have all suffered at the hand of one other. Now, it is time to end this external and internal war, but not by war, but by love.

And life went on for decades. Stories of love, hope, and tragedy consumed her every moment. Her children grew old, and had families and moved away. They, too, would one day fight their own battles to protect their families from harm.

And Marguerite? She died a widow, alone, yet content with her discovery. The beautiful discovery that family is a gift that one should treasure close to their heart, and that no matter what, everyone deserves forgiveness...even the one who spoke with a snake.

CHAPTER FIVE:
MEMORIES AND MEMORY

"Salem?" It was the tender simplicity of the question that brought her back from her state of unawareness. "Come on, where *are* you?"

That, on the other hand, was the high-pitched whining of a very hyperactive four-year-old. It was becoming tedious, this game of 'hide and seek.' The boredom creeped up like the shadow of the door when it was opened.

It was nearing the passing of the hour, and poor, dear little Elizabeth had yet to find her. Dear God, she prayed, what a blessing it would be to be saved from this blasted *nightmare*.

Tick tock, tick tock, does time ever really run out?

She heard her sister scurry around the kitchen, opening cabinets and drawers, as if it were possible to find anyone in those tiny locations. With a blatant sigh she got up from her hiding place in the laundry dumbwaiter and sauntered to the living room.

She positioned herself comfortably perched on the sofa armrest and bellowed out a shrill screech. Three...*two...one*. "Salem!"

She rolled her eyes at the innocent look on her sister's face as Elizabeth stared, a disbelieving look etched on her face. "Were you there the *whole* time? I looked there at least twelve times!"

Salem smirked at the naïve expression and started walking away. "*Oh yes*, I was always there. I can turn invisible, didn't you know?"

Elizabeth was ogling at her retreating form, standing dumbfounded in shock.

I know things that you could only dream of imagining.

She had graced the home's residents with her vivid presence ever since the day she had stepped foot in this home. In a contradictory argument, it would have been stated that she both loved and despised living here.

But she supposed it was better than being under the supervision of *Erham's Correctional Facility*'s "eager" staff. She climbed the narrow old stairs up to the third level, where the ancient attic that would always unravel secrets and mysteries was.

The smell of lemongrass and sage mingled with an odd, musty scent that revealed the building's apparent age. Gracious displays of trinkets and antique furniture were scattered haphazardly around the room, leaving almost no space to walk around. She somehow managed to maneuver through the tricky maze of vast items to a dusty window where the city could be observed below.

The mysteries of this world are for you to discover, when you are ready.

The house used to be a Church, a very long time ago. Nothing remained of the original sanctuary but the grand yet silent bells; the bells, which once likely chimed loudly to indicate the beginning of a new hour, a new opportunity, no longer give that reassurance.

The inevitable sounds of street cars and people below were a certain sign that evening was quickly approaching, and families would soon be gathering for a well-earned supper. Not too far away, one could see a rather tall lookout tower, no doubt remains from the Medieval Ages.

It was not large in size, but extremely narrow in width. There was no doubt that it had stood forgotten for years. The place was likely falling apart on the inside, much like many other buildings in London. It appeared to be constructed majorly of stone, but gave off a strange greenish hue, almost as if it was a mystical passage-way to another realm, tempting her to open its vast possibilities.

You are an enigma, a puzzle and a secret to be
left unsolved.

Salem turned away from the window and decided it would be best if she began to prepare supper. Afterall, Rosalee would soon be home, and exhausted after a long day with the lawyers. She deserved a break after losing her husband so few months ago.

If it had not been for the family's wealth and status, both herself and Rosalee would have had to begin working. They did lose the maid, however, meaning that Salem took over the tiresome job of housekeeper and cook while Rosalee took care of their worrisome situation with the businesspeople.

Isn't it funny how we often will time to go by faster, but
when a single terrible instance occurs and our lives are

*turned inside out, we wish for nothing more than a
moment to break?*

She began to maneuver through the room, until a flash of light caught her attention. She looked at the small mirror in the corner of the room, perplexed, but saw no movement. Perhaps it was simply the reflection of her necklace on the surface of the mirror, or a street car's flashing lights. Quite unsurprisingly, many odd things happen in London, yet this was different somehow.

*Moments... just moments; moments when the veil between
the real and unreal parts. If you're open to them, you might
not miss them.*

Her curiosity, ever prevailing, led her to sit at the windowsill and observe for several moments. It was only when she leaned against the glass to get a better view that something very strange began to happen.

The tower began to glow ominously, a strange nebulous colour slowly expanding around its surface. Then, there was a slow, dreadful moan, almost as if the tower was tired of the activity and wished to do nothing more but rest. Yet it was forced to keep on going with the arduous task of standing upright, until it no longer could.

With another low groan, the building began to tremble and crumble, falling down, down, down, until nothing remained but a vast ruin of stone bricks shadowed by a layer of dust.

*Down, down, down... We always go down, and sometimes,
we get up.*

If someone could have seen the look on her face as she watched in awe as the catastrophe occurred, they would have laughed; but she would not have found it funny.

Salem immediately left the cramped room, descending the wooden stairs and grabbing her coat as she opened the front door. Her hands trembled as she hastily buttoned up her red coat and sprinted the few blocks to the location of the fall. She looked ahead and saw smoke emerging from the surrounding area.

If she could just pass the crowded post office foyer and round the corner, she would arrive at the scene. Bumping into an elderly fellow and getting strange looks from the passersby, she couldn't fathom why no one else was attending to the disaster.

As she turned around the corner, she came to a sudden halt and did a double take. There was nothing there but a forlorn bench and a dead tree. The whole area was just a cobblestone plane, with nothing but small dust clouds emerging as people walked to and fro.

We try so hard and get so far, and then we meet a cross-roads where we can choose to remain or continue going.

Delusions and mistakes; surely she was just tired that day. Yes, most certainly. After all, she had been distracted and stressed with the business of life. It was nothing more than a mirage, or perhaps a figment of her already wild imagination, a dream.

She always had a creative mind, and she could have easily been carried off by fantasies. But... it felt *so real.* Nonetheless, one cannot dwell on mysteries forever, and for the time being she had to focus on her priorities. When things got sorted out, she vowed to try to solve the mystery of the falling tower; to her, that was the best course of action.

What does confusion cause, my darling? Well, chaos of course, but surely you of all people know that.

She didn't understand many things about this world. For one, it was always changing and ever evolving, as if it was trying very hard to become a certain way. She could see it in the way that people desired to change the world too, always innovating and distracting themselves with new ideas and scientific breakthroughs.

They busied themselves so much, and eventually learned so much about life and the world around them, that they forgot to pursue an education in learning about themselves. They become disconnected; wanderers, searching for an answer that could not be found in a book or in an experiment. And soon enough, when anxiety, dread, and emptiness came, they asked themselves why they were only the shell of the person they once were.

We cannot continue the pursuit of happiness, and really have great passion for anything, unless we are truly one with ourselves. Unless we are wholly balanced mentally, physically, emotionally, and spiritually, we will always be looking for answers, *and* questions, that we didn't know we had.

Who are we when we strip off the labels we identify with and the titles we were given by others?

She sat at the shabby table with eyes fixated on the cracked glassware and chipped edges of the *pretty* china. Delicate, flowery napkins with frayed edges were folded on a stack to her right. On the center of the table lay a golden ring set with a single black-encrusted diamond.

She had waited too long to decide her path. While seventeen seemed rather young to be married, their financial situation had been pushing for it since the *incident* nearly two years ago.

A terrible thing it is, to be forced to do something you know
will only bring you misery for the rest of your life.

She remembered that day as clearly as she remembered the day she witnessed *the collapse*, as both days had caused her to question her sanity. It was winter when it happened; the snow was muddy and the cold air crisp and biting.

Jonathan had proposed to her nearly six months ago, after coming to know her through Rosalee's clerk in her new boutique store. It was not quite uncommon for couples to have arranged marriages, or to marry before getting to know each other.

That is yet another subject that had her baffled, as one would think that with the promise to "love one another until the end of their lives," people would be more considerate of their options. Commitment was not something Salem would ever take lightly; she did not believe anyone should. Promises could not be broken without hurting others too. She could not bring herself to choose, so she didn't. Or at least, she didn't pick one of the two most apparent options. One would think that a "yes" or "no" would suffice to answer most questions, but in reality, everything depends.

Everything depends on the people, the time, the place, the weather, one's emotions at the time, and countless other factors. There is no easy answer to any of life's challenging problems; there is only the decision to do everything in your power to find the answer that helps you become the person you were meant to be.

The next time anything as peculiar as the previous incident occurred was about two years after the tower's collapse. She had been out running errands; as life became more and more difficult and busy with domestic issues and financial problems, she had been tasked with holding the family together. As dysfunctional as Rosalee, Elizabeth and herself were, they were still a family, and she loved them.

Salem pulled her long, midnight blue trench coat around her as the biting wind pulled at her. Her long, dark hair whipped wildly as she made her way to her destination. She was relieved when she arrived at the warm bakery and began to browse the aisles for goods. After making an acceptable amount of purchases, she stopped by the grocer next door and got her hands on an abundance of fresh vegetables and dried fruits.

She placed everything in a large knapsack, which she threw over her shoulder before diving straight into the vicious icy battle. She moved quickly but was cautious, as the ice was wicked that time of year and she would not accept an injury. The streets were devoid of the usual plethora of busy shoppers, except for the few beggars who lay shivering in alleys, seeking shelter that no one would ever provide.

She took a shortcut, cutting through a garden and into a large, stone courtyard that had glistening crystals of ice running down its walls. The phenomena caught her eye. Shielded from the wind, she paused a moment to look up and admire the beauty of winter. Sunlight on ice, reflections, freezing cold, foggy breath, nothingness; they made up her world.

Until…fire. Fire; blazing hot streaks of the scorching element flew up in pillars around her. The ice melted, and the water pooling at her feet was burning and evaporating quickly. The heat rose and enveloped her in its anger. The warmth chased away the bitter cold, and replaced it with its burning passion and endless need for action.

The anger grew from her fear, and the flames washed over her like a wave, purifying her from any imperfections. It melted her skin and her muscles lost their form, fusing together into a mass of distorted flesh on the bones of her corpse. She feared the cold no more.

When she awoke, she saw white. But it was not the perfect white that one would expect to see waking up in Heaven. This white was speckled with grey streaks, and cracks of blackness ran across its surface. It seemed…dirty and worn. It was as if it had grown tired of being the perfect, clean surface of reassuring purity, and had become something more feasible…more *real*.

A hand was gently slapping her face, startling her from her staring. She turned to her left and saw the blurry figure of a nurse staring down at her. The nurse checked her over, before explaining her situation in a soft voice that did nothing to lessen the blow of the shock that came when realizing her predicament.

Two months, the nurse said. She had been in a coma for two months. She had fallen after slipping on some ice, and was found and brought to the hospital. She sustained a brain injury, and it would affect her for the rest of her life.

All it takes is a single moment, to save or break a life.

At first, she had wondered why her family never came to see her. She was alone, alone in a large hospital room with not a single soul to speak to. She realized soon enough that the truth behind their absence was that they no longer cared for a burden.

Orphan; she was always the orphan, because she would forever carry her terrible burden alone. She was remembering now; she was remembering her past lives. Families love one another because they see each other for who they really are. Without each other, they would have no hope or strength. But unfortunately, not all family members cared enough, and that was the case with hers.

She felt that in some way, this was a punishment for the way she treated others in her time as the Egyptian queen. Or perhaps, it was Eve's punishment, and a lesson against betrayal. Her existence felt like an endless ride of ups and downs, like joys and traumas, or inspiring dreams and devastating nightmares. In all totality, *life was a beautiful and terrible thing.*

You lived with hope, but died in despair. What is optimism for life worth, if you only dread death when it arrives?

A week later, Rosalee arrived with little Elizabeth in tow. She ranted on with a ridiculous story about how the weather prevented her from coming to visit her ward, as the doors had been frozen shut. Salem would've told her that this was impossible, since the doors were shielded from the weather by the position of the arch, but she couldn't speak. She was going to be living with her great-aunt now. Far out in the county, in a tiny cottage, she would remain supervised and protected, too far away to be a part of their lives anymore.

Everyone will tell you they love and care about you if you have something to offer them, but remember, everybody lies sometimes.

Her aunt was stern, but was willing to give her a chance because she knew Salem was trying. The problem was that Salem wasn't always the one in control of her mind. Her thoughts would wander and she would begin to drift away, into a place she named euphoria. Her pupils would dilate rapidly and no amount of noise would bring her back. It was in moments like these where Auntie

Anthea would lose her temper and lash out at the girl. Long fingernails would strike Salem's face, and bruises from her aunt's cane would cover her body. And in her illness, she would refuse to eat any morsel of food, and she would waste away more and more.

Lessons in the morning: literature, arithmetic, history, and the piano. In the afternoon, there would be chores and preparing meals. The evenings were her free time to read, go on a walk, or knit useless garments of clothing.

She fell into this rigid routine and lived with the fear of failure, the fear of pain and rejection. She always did her absolute best, but somehow no matter how hard she tried, it was never enough. She could never seem to please anyone... everyone.

You try so, so hard, yet you're always one step behind in this cruel game of life. Perhaps, we are meant to follow life's path and see where it takes us first?

Thousands of years ago, she would have prayed to God above for forgiveness, and begged with all of her heart to be given another chance at life. But now, in this life, she was beyond believing that she was worthy of mercy. She accepted every blow as a reminder of her inadequacies.

Over and over again, her mind betrayed her. She sinned, and her hopes were thrown back in her face. She was dying inside and out, over and over and over again. On the outside, she was a girl, but inside, she was a rotten, gory monster of decaying flesh, festering with crawling insects and bloody scratches.

Don't be so hard on yourself; you are only what you perceive yourself to be, and your opinion is biased.

She sat amongst the rocks. The large boulders that rested at the side of the pond were sturdy and solid. They had a strong foundation and were mighty and sure of themselves, the opposite of her.

One year ago today, she had fallen, and her life had changed forever. From then on, no one ever trusted her, and she lost her freedom. As she stared out into the fields of overgrown grass and daisy flowers, she thought about all of the things about her life that made it special.

She was always different, no matter where she was nor whatever life she lived. She was special. She was an enigma. Whether it be through bravery, fortitude, intelligence, hard work or kindness, she was special. She cared so much about everything, so much so that her mind never stopped. Her eyes raced side to side rapidly as she entered euphoria, and then, she was trapped in a flashback.

Stone falling around her, fire rising up, black rings, abandonment, loss, failure, and pain were all she knew. She never had a head injury, because she had never fallen. They had found her in the freezing courtyard, alone, muttering incomprehensible nonsense, and immediately brought her to the hospital.

Weeks went by. Diagnosis…schizophrenia. White rooms and doctors, silence or insanity; she was either mute, or screaming, never anything in between. Lost cause; she would have a short and difficult life.

Sometimes, she would see visions of different people in her mind. As she lay in bed, other women would visit her, pass by her and whisper secrets in her ear. In time, she would realize that these women were other versions of her, perhaps living simultaneously but in a different reality. She yearned to leave this reality, reach far beyond the edge of this dimension, and meld into another.

Not everything is what it seems, but sometimes, not knowing the truth saves us from the pain of our reality.

The meadow came back into her view. Colours melded together and black spots distorted her vision. Above her the crows flew; omens. Black eyes stared at her, and she watched back in fear. Flocks were forming and they approached her.

Crows gathered like spectators, and flew above observing with menacing eyes. To win the championship, she would have to get away fast enough. *Run.* Wherever she ran they followed, and soon enough she was surrounded at the other side of the pond. Beaks pecked at her clothes and knotted hair. Her arms smacked at the offensive forms, fighting to save herself.

Save me from myself.

She stumbled and fell roughly to the rocky ground. Scratches littered every corner of her flesh, and she lost the strength to fight the monsters around her. In her peripheral vision, she watched as the crows shape-shifted into creatures of black robes and sharp nails.

They dragged her to the water's edge, and on her side, she looked at her reflection. Or at least, what would have been her reflection if she was actually there. Nothingness. With one last look at the sky, she rolled into the water and into its murky depths.

When the automatic impulse to get air kicked in, she struggled, but jagged hands held her down in the water. She screamed, and the last bit of oxygen left her lungs.

When she awoke, she was greeted with the familiar site of her asylum door, and the beautifully imperfect whiteness of the room.

You don't always really know what you think you know.

CHAPTER SIX:

BLOOD AND WATER

She once knew a girl who made all the wrong choices, and ruined everything she once stood for. This girl was destined to be led by darkness, and darkness was what she became. Born the heir to one of the darkest, most malicious counts in all of Europe, she was expected to take up his image. What she did, however, was much, much worse.

Pray tell me, what did I do to make you believe that?

It was the summer of 1876, and all was well. Adelaine spent her time helping their maid Tula tidy and cook, as well as sneaking off to the secret cellar by the baker's shop to read *Moby Dick* and other fantastic books.

She always looked for excuses to slip away from the mundane order of daily life in order to search for an adventure. Her mother never approved of her stubbornness and curious nature, and would scold her and tell her to grow up. As an upper-class woman who was expected to already be married and have children, she had far more opportunities in her life than the impoverished, lower-class ladies.

While frowned upon, it was not entirely impossible for her to be able to pursue a basic education, so being seen with a book would not get her into trouble. However, of late, many men had been attempting to court her, and she was far from impressed. Of course, being a woman of decent status, many knew her name and wished to gain her family's wealth through marriage.

Among them were Smith, Archer, Bertram, and Rodolpho, and none of these young men had anything good to their name. Rich though they were, they were blasphemous, immoral, and vile bastards who fed on pain and dishonourable, dirty actions. Even worse, they were all comrades, and no one would dare to go up against them because they held greater power.

Oh, how I wonder what it would be like to be loved for
something more than my body or wealth? Truly a wonder
it is, to find a man who loves me for me.

It was mere minutes after sunrise when the sound of horses trotting by the shop woke her up from her deep slumber. Inside the cellar she lay, going over the previous day's events and laughing at her ever-present luck. The thrill of adrenaline was what she lived for, and she would seek it until her bones were too old to carry her.

She recalled darting around town the night previous, escaping the common enemy after having provoked them in their cave. Men were foolish when they were intoxicated, but easy to manipulate all the same. She had convinced a group of young gentlemen to fight in her defense and knock some sense into Smith after he had continuously harassed her the weeks previous. He suffered a good thrashing, but when his drunk friends, Bertram and Archer, showed up, they took one look at her and immediately began the pursuit.

Adrenaline in your veins, blood rushing to your head, the strain in your muscles, and the ache in your bones are the first taste of a life of thrills and unexpected endeavours.

She had searched for a good place to hide from the violent drunkards pursuing her. While not quite the most peculiar adventure she had inadvertently gotten herself into, it still wasn't quite her ideal evening.

While usually able to hold her ground against an insolent man in her shadow, something that Smith did drove her over the edge, and she had wanted an extra bit of help in her revenge.

When her precious silver necklace had gone missing shortly after a war of words with the man, she had immediately suspected it was he who stole it, just to spite her. Any other jewelry item she would have shrugged off as unimportant as she had so many; however, this one was no ordinary piece.

It was a rather peculiar necklace, given to her by her late father and crafted by Louis Arnette, a famous jeweler and silversmith. Not to say that her father was incredibly strange, but his taste was most certainly odd, to say the least. The necklace was constructed with many thin silver strings that joined together at one point to hold a single charm, a spider. Most fathers would present their daughters with gifts representing innocence and joy, such as bluebird charms or pearl necklaces, yet Adelaine received a gift representing magic far more sinister.

Nonetheless, it was the last thing her father bestowed to her before his tragic passing, and she held it very close to her heart.

She promised herself that she would find it immediately, and never let it go as soon as it was returned to her.

How far would you go, if you realized that limits did not really exist?

After getting her revenge on Smith, she retrieved her necklace from his coat pocket and placed it around her neck. The weight of the silver on her chest and the sinister energy of the piece was strong, and she loved every part of it. And just like a flash of lightning, she was gone, running from the people who wished to control her and make her fall apart.

Strong women, you will not crack under pressure when they expect you to be feeble and weak. Rather, you will lift up your fears and burdens, holding them high above your head, and shout out to the world that you are a conqueror and you are a queen.

Climbing out of the old, dust-covered trapdoor, she was rewarded by a loud creaking noise and the frantic garble of some flustered chickens nearby. The cellar was located at the back of the baker's home, and much like a storm cellar, wasn't used for many other purposes.

Being practically abandoned, and far from most prying eyes thanks to its position at the edge of town, it was her ideal getaway. As per usual, she began her journey to the outskirts of the surrounding forest, through the winding narrow roads and past all the towering trees. The ground was not even, but rather formed on rolling hills; the surrounding area was encased in a ring of jagged mountains and steep cliffs.

They always gave foreigners the impression that the town was protected by a God-given impenetrable wall, obscuring enemies from finding a safe passage in. She, however, saw it as a means of keeping them in, a prison.

*One may see a treasure and one may see scum, just like
one may see a hellish outcome or a paradise overdone.*

From the highest feeble branches of a large weeping willow, she could see her destination, an early-times, dark, gothic castle surrounded by a relatively tall, menacing iron fence. The vast gate at its entrance gleamed promisingly in the early sunrise, and the thick metal features on the hardwood doors reflected the sun's rays like a welcoming promise.

While this was not an unfamiliar sight, the beauty and forlorn majesty of the familiar estate entranced her with reasonable satisfaction. The castle before her stood firm and mighty in a way that enticed her to believe it would go up against any chaos and any fear.

It took mere minutes to approach the grand entrance, and with no guards or servants whatsoever, she let herself in and navigated her way to the entrance hall. Inside laid a stone-cold statue of a curious man with a curved nose, dark eyes and rather pointed teeth. The cape he donned was long, and would be flowing were he not still. The long staff clasped in his left hand was adorned with a gleaming, blood-red jewel, being the only feature with colour. His presence would have been terrifying had she not already seen it dozens of times before, and she found herself quickly gliding up the marble grand staircase to the second storey.

There was a torch burning on the wall to her left, and as the light caught her eye, she froze and remembered what fire really meant. Fire burned, fire destroyed, fire was a weapon that had burned her before. Though not real, being in her madness so to speak, it never completely left her consciousness, and it made her feel weak.

Snapping out of her trance, she began to hear shrieks and distressed crying. Walking down the hall, the numerous portraits of long-deceased previous occupants followed her every step, as they were painted in such a way to terrify their observers. At the end of the hall stood a single short, pitch-black door with a silver handle.

She approached it and slowly opened the entrance, to be greeted with a not-so-shocking scene of utter chaos. The room was free from any furniture except a single cot pushed to the side, and in the corner laid a raven-haired girl, bawling her eyes out.

"Marya," she whispered soothingly, "what happened now?"

"He did it again!" the girl wailed loudly, causing the room to vibrate with the heightened noise. She sat hunched over, with her knees drawn to her chest and her arms covering her face as she shuddered and sobbed.

Adelaine slowly kneeled in front of her and imposed a common question that she already knew the answer to. "What did he do?"

"He won't leave me alone!" The anger was evident in her voice as her head snapped up and wild bloodshot eyes met hers. The veins under her eyes were blackened, and the prominent veins in her limbs continued to rapidly darken, giving her pale figure a sickening effect. "He won't get out of my head, Addy."

Adelaine grasped Marya's hands in her own and took note of the relentless shaking and frailty of the spindly fingers, and the gruesome contrast of black and white. "Pray with me." She took out a simple, wood rosary and they recited the prayers, their voices cracking at times but never faltering.

And as always it ended with the same statement, said by Adelaine alone. "I believe in you and know you are strong enough to defeat your demons. Now believe in yourself, because only you can win your battles."

With determination set in Marya's eyes, Addy was confident that she would be able to leave now, with the danger past. Until a distant look entered her friend's eyes and brought with it the promise that today would be the day that the end would begin to unfold.

Marya was no ordinary young woman. When she was young, she had a happy life with an older brother by two years, a kind-hearted mother, and a stern father, all of whom were very supportive. But then, on her seventh birthday, mysterious events began to unfold.

The medicine lady and her many apprentices, who were all well acquainted with the sweet, charming child, were suddenly overcome with a terrible sense of foreboding and insight. Being less than a year younger than Marya, Adelaine recalled the events exactly.

The medicine lady warned of a storm coming; bad times were near, and soon a curse would fall upon the people of this land, and would be unrelenting until the child died. Marya was cursed with the burden of carrying her father's sin, whom she later found out was a murderer of many and a wicked abuser of his power, being born the heir to an incredibly wealthy aristocrat.

Obviously perturbed and somewhat mistrusting of the sudden change of perspective in regard to the powerful family, the townspeople did nothing to acknowledge the proposed revelation.

Before sunset, the girl's mother was found outside the apothecary in a pool of blood, dead by a brain hemorrhage. The following day, her brother was discovered by a few local schoolboys fallen from the branch of a lone cypress tree. This impact was fatal, breaking his neck mercilessly. Accidents they said, tragic accidents. Both funerals took place on the same day, in the town square where all the citizens attended.

At the front of the crowd was a little girl in a red lace dress, with black bows in her hair and tears in her eyes. She was not so young that she did not understand what was happening, and when the procession was over she horrified everyone by submitting herself before the medicine lady. Her soft voice was seemingly magnified by the utter stillness of the crowd as she offered, "You can kill me now, if you'd like to."

Then her father was suddenly there, whisking her off to dwell in the dark castle, away from civilization, where she suffered under his wrath for many years. In time, people forgot about the little girl, happy to be far from the "demon child," regardless of whether she was alive or not.

They disregarded the prophecy's encouragement to end her life, and began to ease into lives of suffering, soon forgetting how things were before. They became angrier and cruel, feeding off of the suffering of others. Families began to separate, and many were torn apart. The atmosphere grew darker, and soon abuse and murders were far more common and less despicable than the council's new definition of corrupt.

The greatest struggle was controlling the financial state of the town, as more and more money was being spent on dishonourable entertainment than essential products and goods. The town had become filthy and unkempt, along with its residents.

And all through this, the little girl was suffering horrors far worse than death. Her father became enraged and insanity took hold of him, and he began to do everything in his power to murder his own kin.

She soon learned to hide, to escape her reality of nightmares by shutting herself down and locking herself away so she would never have to see his face. This went on for many months, before one day a hunter found his body washed up on shore from the stream that flowed outside the town.

There were no fatal injuries on him, but upon closer inspection, the coroner discovered that his eyes were red and would not close, no matter their efforts. While enough to rouse their suspicions, there was no feasible proof to claim the child guilty for any of her family's deaths, and no one would dare test the theory by going to find out. Bad luck was what they called it; the family was wealthy, and surely had many enemies because of it. It couldn't have been more than that.

And sure enough they were right. For twelve years, no other mishap or odd event took place. The townspeople were still more miserable than before the events of the horrible tragedy, though, but were seldom living normal lives. Besides the nagging thought in the back of the minds of the few that could have bothered to be concerned with the whereabouts of the long-absent child, no one gave a second thought to the mysterious disappearance of the once seven-year-old. All except one.

After witnessing the events leading up to the final death, Adelaine began to busy herself with trying to discover the meaning behind the occurrences. Young though she was at the time, she desired to do good and help another person who had also suffered the loss of loved ones.

It took her an entire year to work up the courage to venture out into the woods and travel the long journey to the castle, but when she got her first glimpse of the towering, eerie spires she immediately turned around and ran back.

Courage, you are an anomaly that only truly unique people stumble upon.

It wasn't until she was fourteen that she tried again. Making it to the entrance and finding the gate bolted shut and the tall, jagged iron fence too dangerous and impossible to climb, she turned back once more.

She considered fetching a grappling hook to climb over it, but when she returned home to find it, her mother discovered her plan and panicked. Bringing to light her reckless persona, her mother vowed to do everything in her power to keep an eye on her daughter and prevent her from ever venturing out again.

You can never win as a parent, because too much freedom may get your children hurt, but over-protectiveness is a recipe for rebellion.

Adelaine felt her mother was just being paranoid. After losing her husband several months before what became known as "the First Death" of three, she couldn't fathom the idea of losing anyone else. Addy's elder brother James was forced to find work in the greater city several miles away, despite their fairly decent savings, and her mother and herself were left alone. While always busying herself with chores and gatherings with other ladies, her mother was lonely, and more so than ever concerned with her daughter's well-being.

Understanding, albeit still frustrated with everything else going on, Addy tried her best to appease her only guardian from then on forth.

I love you too.

When she finally did meet Marya for the first time, she was horrified at the insanity of her life. But the initial shock wore off very quickly, because upon recalling her previous life, she noted the familiarity and came to a frightening realization. The parallels between Marya Lazarescu and herself, Adelaine Moore, were astronomical.

> *Staring into the candle flame as the wax dripped along the sides, she could think only of the elegance of the crystals on the courtyard walls, and how they were likely the last real thing she ever saw.*

Marya suffered from intense delusions and traumas as a result of her father's abuse. She was not in her right mind the majority of the time, but she loved her friend Addy with all of her heart, and was forever grateful for her sacrifice to help her. Addy helped her through everything, understanding the terrifying madness that was the result of mental illness.

Outside the falling tower and inside the sturdy castle walls, Adelaine put together the pieces of her own broken soul, as well as Marya's. The strange likenesses reawakened the most vulnerable parts of her spirit, and she eventually left the desire for thrill in pursuit of clarity and peace of mind.

It was a terrifying thing to watch her friend over the years, as she suffered from wounds that went beyond flesh and blood. Marya's wounds were deep inside, and scars covered every crevice of her mind. She felt the illness eating away at her mind and the psychosis grew in power and she slipped away more and more each day.

Agatha, the wisest medicine woman, had warned of the coming of the demon princess. When Adelaine had gone to her looking for help, the elder had explained that Marya would not live past her twenty-first birthday, and that when the illness took over, her cursed powers would force her into a state of uncontrollable rage.

Nothing would stop her from taking the lives of the civilians when the bottle exploded and the uncontainable was released.

A foreshadow into the future: you'll have to do things you don't always want to do in life, and it may be terribly inopportune.

Marya could barely focus anymore. When Addy spoke to her, she would have to talk incredibly slowly, and use a great amount of articulation to get through to her friend. Marya was incredibly intelligent and gifted, but her illness prevented her from using her gifts for good, or at all really.

White rooms and doctors with white coats and masks that talked in slow, reassuring voices that a child would be annoyed at, were her ever-present visitors. She wasn't stupid, she was just insane. And you know what, all the best people have a few screws loose, so what does it matter?

Marya's anger emerged as her self-control weakened. She would lash out and throw things for no reason, and her patience was non-existent. Addy knew her time was running out. As much as it pained her to do so, she devised a plan that would bring a painless death to her closest friend.

The evening before the twenty-first birthday of young Miss Lazarescu, Addy prepared a steaming cup of chamomile tea. The soothing herbs, coupled with valerian root, would place her friend into a peaceful slumber. And from there, the poison would enter her veins and destroy her from the inside out, silently.

Poison is easily hidden, but gives rise to indisputable results that can often not be reversed in time.

Not all things go as planned. Unfortunately for Addy, her plan wasn't very elaborate or intricate, and Marya saw right through it. The betrayal pushed her over the edge, and within minutes of shouting at her now sworn enemy, she cracked. Her powers were unleashed to their full potential for the first time in nearly two decades, and her confusion swirled in spirals around her.

The sight was terrifying. Without moving a muscle, Marya summoned the winds into the house, and they tore through anything in their way. Her eyes glowed white, and a terrible wave of fury washed over her and targeted the only other person in the room. The energy consumed every fibre of Addy's being, and the evil attacked her inside and out. It dug deep into her mind and dragged out her darkest memories, failures, and fears. She lay on her back, gasping for breath, and as her vision faded, she heard a door open and slam shut as the empowered villainess dove into the night.

The cave was dark and eerie, sending chills down her spine as she sought out warmth and light. She felt the wall's jagged features as she used them to guide her to the way out. She stumbled on the roots of the dirt floor, and trembled as the isolation started getting to her. She was alone, in a small space, unable to see anything. Panic set in. She staggered along faster, trying to escape the hellhole as soon as possible. At the end of the tunnel, she saw a light, and her heart jumped at the flicker of hope that ignited within her.

If she could only get there faster, she would be okay. The distance became smaller and smaller as she neared the end, until the unexpected happened: she fell. She was falling down a hole, deep into the depths of the Earth. When she landed, she felt no pain or discomfort. She got up and made out her surroundings. The bottom of the pit was barely a square meter, and the walls were too smooth to climb up,

Being alone, being abandoned, that was her worst fear. Claustrophobia only added to that fear, as it reminded her of the way the blanket of darkness always tightened around her, acting as her only comfort. Darkness was the static thing in her life, and it should have been her friend. In the bottom of the pit, she wept and wept until her eyes grew tired and closed. Lonely was who she was, and the darkness was her only friend, because the light had only made her find her shadow.

Waking up on the demolished wooden floor of the castle, she noticed that many hours had passed; the sun was rising across the horizon. She was scared now, tainted, and she wished to get revenge on the person who made her live her worst nightmare. She no longer cared for Marya; she was nothing more than another villain.

Our perspectives change so quickly, when we realize what we believe to be the truth.

Adelaine got up and cleared the fallen pieces of wood off of her. As a habit, she gripped her necklace, as a comfort. However, she felt something was off, and when she gazed down at her necklace, she noticed something incredible.

The necklace glowed with a reddish hue, and inside the spider's mouth was a beautiful ruby. When Adelaine touched the gem, a red-coloured substance began covering her arm, and the rest of her body. She screamed in surprise and tried to remove the substance that so closely resembled blood, to no avail. When it reached her eyes, she closed them, and was fully engulfed in the liquid.

It changed her, she felt it. She felt power surge within her, a magic that came only as a result of the incredible work of a magnificent spirit. Marya gave her a blessing that day, but with it, was a curse that far outweighed the benefits of the power. She became inhuman, or at least, to the others she would be. They would fear her, and it broke her heart. Later, when they would come for her, she wouldn't fight them out of anger, but out of fear. She was lost, and she didn't want to die a death of a monster; it was never her choice to become this way.

When she arrived at the village after recovering from her transformation, she was greeted with the sight of weeping woman and furious men. In the center of the square lay twelve people, dead. There was no cause identified; according to the medicine women, it could only be the work of terrible dark magic.

Many people came to the conclusion that it must indeed been the work of the demon child, until Agatha reminded them of the impossibility. Addy was confused, but as she gazed at the corpses that laid in the square, one particular body caught her attention. Marya. Her best friend was dead.

Her scream tore through the town before she could stop it from bursting out. With her grief emerged her power, and dark mist rose around her as she fell to her knees and wept over the body of the girl she had come to see as a sister, despite their difficulties.

She had been found out, she realized. They would suspect her now, seeing as she was the only other person ever seen with magical abilities. Shrieks of terror rose around her. People were always afraid of the things they didn't understand. She forced herself to get up and run for the woods, but she didn't enter alone. Her pursuers were close at her heels.

She created dark masses of smoke rising in clouds around her as she ran. When grimy fingers reached out in the dark, they turned black and crumbled into ashes on the ground. If she saw them, the power surged within her, and they let out screams before being suffocated in their own blood. She really was a monster, but they weren't innocent either.

With curved, menacing knives and flaming pitchforks, they ran in her pursuit, not stopping to help their fallen comrades. Adelaine fled through and across forest grounds, dark and difficult to follow in the night. Knots of roots and sharp-tipped rocks made her fall more than once, and her dress tore on the intruding branches and thorny bushes. Her hands were stained with a thick, coppery substance that could only be identified as blood, and her skin was blackened and charred in places where flaming arrows had met their mark.

At the edge of the forest was a stream, ominous and sparkling in the moonlight. Peering into her own reflection, she saw the numerous cuts that adorned her face and the filthy, wild hair that whipped around as the wind grew ever more violent.

Upon closer inspection, she realized that her eyes no longer held their calming, blue reassurance, but almost looked deranged and a more sinister, faded grey. With nowhere else to run, her hands gripped the edge of the bank, and she listened to the sound of angry voices and clamouring footsteps.

She fell into the water, and as the natural instinct to get oxygen kicked in, scaly hands held her down. The stream or the pond, neither were desirable places to be.

Everything felt surreal, and she realized, as her heart clenched, that she didn't want to live anymore. She was so tired of running from the person she had become, that she figured she would never be able to be the girl she once knew.

Before, there was darkness, and there was light. Now, she realized that darkness never really existed, for it was an absence of light. There would always be light in this world, whether a lot, or nearly none at all. In her life, the light had been almost sucked away entirely, leaving her alone and afraid.

But in reality, there was always still some light in her, because a person cannot truly be evil entirely. In the back of her mind, she could recall a time when she was known as the light, and she soared high above and illuminated a path for those around her to see.

She had not been tainted with the evil of the world, but had been more like an innocent child, passionate and curious. In her attempt to save others, she lost herself, and now she would pay the price for becoming the one thing she was never supposed to be.

Behind her she could hear a voice. "We found her, Rodolpho. We found your pretty little bloody bride."

Snickers and cold laughter enveloped the atmosphere. and she felt the darkness return to her.

A snide voice spoke out. "So princess, you going to come quietly, or do we kill you here?"

She felt the fury begin to bubble within, and suddenly she was not afraid, but mad. She stood up, still gazing at the murky depths below, and turned around slowly as her hands clenched tightly into fists. "You know what, gentlemen? I think we'll just end these little charades right here. What do you say, time to have some fun?"

She smirked wickedly at the cowards who surrounded her, seeing her as prey during hunting season. They would soon see that she wasn't the hunted, but the huntress.

Madness; a term used to describe chaotic behaviour, and also, exactly what happened next. Black flames rose from the palms of her hands and encircled her like cobras stalking their target. Her eyes turned black, and heat rose from the earth and enveloped the scene. Addy let out a blood-curdling shriek as she released all the fear and pain within her spirit.

She felt it inside of her; its desire to kill and destroy everything, every soul that had ever done her harm. It desired to shred the enemy to pieces, leaving no mercy for the wicked. She was deranged, and this was her madness.

It overwhelmed her, and she wished to end everything at once. But then, she heard a voice from within, a calming voice much like a young girl. "Addy, please don't do this. Don't make the same mistake Marya made. You can be good again. Just remember how this all started."

Adelaine saw the vision. Around her soared a thousand angels, as well as many demons. The beings of light sang angelically, and with swords adorned with bright gold and glistening with light, they drove away the evil.

In front of her stood a little girl with a lit match clasped in her tiny hand. She smiled and walked up to Addy. She had sparkling blue eyes and flowing golden locks for hair. Her bare feet did not touch the ground as she walked, and her white robe shimmered in the sudden overwhelming light.

When she reached Addy, she took the elder's hand in hers and whispered, "Hold onto the light, for in the darkest of times, we can only hope and fight to remain good."

When Addy took the offered match, the girl began to fade away. Adelaine reached out to her, only to find nothing solid in her grasp. When she blinked, everyone was gone, and there was absolute silence.

She looked around and saw the hunters lying in heaps on the grubby ground; they were asleep. The once rushing stream was entirely still, and no animal called out from the woods. She found in her hand a tiny golden key adorned with a single white pearl.

Before she knew what she was doing, her feet were already in the icy water, and she made no move to prevent herself from walking deeper still. The water felt soothing on her injuries, particularly the many burns she sustained. When her head was submerged underwater, she wondered if she should just end it all. She was not afraid of death, because it was not really death if she just began a new life.

But to commit such an action would be a sin, and she could not bring herself to participate in such an action. She emerged from the murky depths on the other side of the stream and walked on towards the towering mountains many miles ahead. With the dagger she kept in her pocket, she cut some vine off a tree to make a necklace to hold her key, and tied it around her neck.

For many miles, she walked on alone, never looking back at the life she was leaving behind. For now, no animal nor person bothered her or acknowledged her in any way. She was alone in this world.

When she reached a moment where she could walk no longer, she took her place under a shallow oak tree and sat quietly gazing at the beautiful scenery around her. Fatigue took over, and she found herself wishing that she could simply rest in this place forever. The last thing she heard before she fell asleep was the sound of a crow calling in the distance.

Not too long after she fell asleep, she found herself astral projecting and ascending above the trees around her. From above, she saw her body where it lay, broken and battered, yet finally at peace.

She gracefully floated over the ancient, gnarly trees towards the handsome mountains. Reaching them, she took her place on a pointed edge and gazed at the horizon. She heard the calls of the olden wolves as they approached her, and came to rest by her side. At the mountain's peak, there was a small, rustic, wooden cabin. She was drawn to its mystery and simplicity. She made her way up the winding, narrow pathway, which curved dangerously close to the edge. She approached the rough, dark wood door and found it locked. Then she noticed the golden handle with a keyhole slot. She reached for her key, taking it off from around her neck, and inserted it into the slot.

She opened the door and stepped inside the tiny home, where she found a shocking sight. There was nothing in the room but a single wooden stool, with a dark-haired person seated upon it.

"Marya," she forced out of her constricted throat.

"Hello, Addy. I am here to take you home." Marya looked up at her friend with a soft expression, sorrow and regret mixed with understanding and compassion. "It's time for us to start again. We can no longer be happy in this world, because our mission is over," she whispered serenely.

Addy stared at her with questioning eyes. "But you failed your mission, didn't you Marya?"

Her expression melted into something akin to dismay. "Yes, I did. But you didn't. You never let the darkness win, and for that, you will be greatly rewarded."

"But then, what now?"

"Now, you take my hand." She reached out with a translucent hand similar to that of Addy's own spirit body.

Addy felt a surge of familiarity as she truly realized who she was with, her best friend turned enemy. "Marya?"

"Yes, Adelaine?" They clasped hands, feeling the world fade around them.

"I forgive you."

CHAPTER SEVEN:

PARAMOUNT CHILD AND PAINTING SMILES

When life gets interesting, we forget our sorrows and woes,
We brighten our minds and start the journey of letting go.
When the bright light of hope is turned on, we become exuberant
and elated,
Forgetting the gloomy path from which we were taken.

When new beginnings are bestowed upon us in the most unfore-
seen moments in time,
We become delirious with the promise of a sudden adventure and
fly high.
When we become well acquainted with this world and come to
understand its functions,

We gain knowledge and wisdom that would otherwise
be unprecedented.

When we commence the difficult mission of helping others, and
more essentially ourselves,
We learn a many great things and are overwhelmed with revela-
tions and reassuring vows.
When we find out who we truly are, and who we truly wish to be,
We gain a sense of determination and a reason to believe.

When life gives you hardships and far too many reasons to grieve,
Remember who loves you and know you have all the remedies.
When love seems to be fighting to give up and everyone seems
to leave,
Know in your heart that reality is not always what it seems to be.

When you are old and grey and holding on to your last breath,
Don't forget your wonderful experiences and the people you
have met.
When life gets interesting, don't hold back,
Seize the moment and make it always last, so you never go down
the wrong path.

Leave your fears behind you and walk forward into the light and
be reconciled,
Believe in your Father and let nothing ever stop you from being
his paramount child.

Poetry was only one of many gifts he had. Yes, *he.* Adelaine had
been tired of fear and solitude, and wished for a definite change.
She had only ever experienced the world through the eyes of a
woman, and wished to gain some perspective. She wished to live

in a world where she could express herself freely and not have to fall beneath the foot of the dominant gender. In order to discover the true opportunities of life, she had to be free to discover them first. Upon her reincarnation, she discovered that her wish had indeed been granted.

He was born in the flesh, rather than awakening as a child. Early life went by quickly, and no memories emerged until he reached the age in which he would've incarnated in this era. And as expected, the realization that he was truly an infinite soul that reincarnated primarily in the female form was rather terrifying. It was odd, to say the least, to live a life where the lines of gender were blurred.

As he grew older, he discovered self-expression through wearing strange and colourful garments, an art that he was often mocked and questioned for. Many gossiped and implied that he was significantly less *manly* that he should have been, but they didn't understand.

It was strange, because the memories and present contradicted each other, for man and woman were opposites. In time, however, he began to realize that no matter what he felt, the only thing that mattered was finding what lay in his heart. And his heart held many passions.

From flying machines to commendable works of art, he was a man of many talents. He wished to experience the world and learn as much as possible, for it would bring a different kind of fulfillment, one of having accomplished becoming knowledgeable.

One thing he distinguished before beginning the journey of self-empowerment was the difference between knowledge and wisdom, for he knew that no matter how many things he learned, he would still be a fool at heart. A fool he would be, because he was human. And a human embracing the wildest side of life, at that.

Studying is a powerful tool in aiding one's success, but it is not all that life offers. Beyond books, there is a study that can be embraced only through the experience of adventure, real life. For life is not a simple timeline from birth to death, but a rocky journey that aspires to teach us lessons about ourselves and the people around us.

Self-knowledge is one of the most powerful things to study, for it leads to true wisdom in time. Alas, wisdom cannot be obtained through studies, but only through experiences and reflection. When one takes the time to ponder the simplest wonders and imagine the most obscene mysteries, one is awakened to the world of creativity.

It was in his workshop that he explored this dimension. Old diagrams and models lay haphazardly around the room, seemingly having no direction at all. The old patterned wallpaper was peeling and stained in numerous places. Endless stacks of paper and journals covered every spare corner of the room, and an artist's palette and easel were stowed in the cramped space in front of the only window. The man lying in the center of this madness emitted an aura of chaos itself, as if he had embodied it entirely.

When the cuckoo-clock chimed one in the afternoon, the middle-aged man groaned and dragged himself up from the half-hidden wooden floor. He made his way over to his desk and sat in his chair, after removing a stack of feather hats from it and throwing them over his shoulder. He murmured constantly under his breath, reciting a non-stop rant about the numerous problems in the world; and his solutions for them, of course. Retrieving a piece of parchment, he messily wrote out a brief letter with a feather quill that said, "Tomorrow, two o'clock, wear black."

He then made his way to the door, before backtracking to check on his pet salamander, which he found dead. Grabbing it by the tail, he chucked it outside as he made his way to the center of town. He found the nearest lad and instructed him to deliver the letter to *the lady*. The boy took off upon receiving three coins, and the man found himself alone to wander about the city.

He went where the day brought him. He had no obligations, for he had many jobs, all of which were on his own schedule; unless there were death threats, of course, prompting him to finish. Today he helped the local botanist identify what disease was ailing his petunias, met with Flora to help her organize her shop's window display, and instructed the local butcher on what meats were most popular during spring, according to a survey he recorded four weeks ago.

And in between his "working hours," he would do whatever his heart desired. That evening, it entitled eating lamb and buttered bread while observing the streaming water running under a local bridge. This life, he thought, was not about anything other than finding oneself and inspiring others to do the same.

He looked back at the journal once, reciting his poem about the paramount child, and thought about when he was Naamah, fearing a relationship with God. It reminded him of Marguerite, and her love for her children. It was a memory, a story, but it was not a reality. The poem recalled, he believed, a time when it was easy to have faith; a lifetime before there was sin and temptation.

But above all, it reminded him of himself, for though he was not yet reconciled with God, he was living a life of adventure, discovery, and passion. He was embracing life at its greatest potential, and not wasting a moment of time to fear.

He stared at her face with a critical and observant gaze. It was something about the way she looked that threw him off; it distracted him from the task at hand. There she was, sitting peacefully at the makeshift windowsill in his workshop, unwavering in her stare and ever-present despite his odd facial expression.

Then the epiphany came. Ah hah! It was the smile! Her smile described something he could not understand at that time, but would later spend hours pondering. The smile was one of a powerful and mystical being, and he loved how it changed his ideas entirely. Needing time to think, he shooed the woman out, telling her to return in a week. She left confused, but not surprised, as all citizens of the town knew the man for his strange methods.

Running a hand over his beard, he thought and he thought and he thought about the secret he was missing. It was clearly right in front of him, yet he was still clueless. They say the eyes are the way to see the soul, but there must be more to it! Befuddled, the man left his workshop and began walking around town, both to clear his head and hopefully find some answers.

Deep in thought, he failed to pay attention to where he was walking and accidentally bumped into a small figure walking in the opposite direction. Muttering an apology, he continued walking without sparing a glance at the person; that was until he felt a tug at his sleeve. He turned around to see a small girl looking up at him pleasantly. "Excuse me, mister. But you dropped your pocket watch."

She held up the watch, and he did indeed recognize it as his. He thanked the young girl for returning it to him rather than running away with it. Her response was life changing. She beamed up at him, smiling ear-to-ear before saying, "No problem mister. Have a nice day!"

Then she was off and he stared after her, his jaw dropping to the floor. He knew the secret now, he understood the power. And back in his workshop he wrote and wrote, far past the middle of the night and into the early hours of morning.

He spoke now of a power he believed all people had, the power to be brave and kind without losing themselves. And the way he described it was by the way they smile, the way they love and care for others so very much. For the beauty of a smile is a gift that elates others and brings more positivity into the world.

All it takes is a single moment, an exchange of a greeting or an acknowledgement to a passerby, to make their day. One type of smile, in particular, is known for its mystery and allure, for it makes one question the secrets of the spirit. This smile is one that entices you to learn more about that person, and discover how they found out about the secret and how it can change the world.

Beauty is not always in the way one looks, but the contents of one's soul. Many believe the eyes are the gateway into the soul, so a smile is very precious, for it reveals a person's true character. One may believe it strange for another to think of such trivial things, but some people are thinkers, that wish to make a change. Some wish to plant a secret into society, one that might help make people see the beauty of humankind, and that all are equal and deserving of the same opportunities.

She was lucky because she got to experience a life of endless possibilities, but she had to be a man in order for it to be possible. Now she wanted to leave a message, a tiny prodding, that would plant the idea in the minds of men. In the painting, she would illustrate the idea that women too should be free to do the things that only men could do for so long. So she found the one, intelligence and grace, to be the messenger to the world that a secret exists.

She painted the woman in a dark setting that illustrated the darkness of the world, and made her the light in a place in need of hope. Her kindness and her wisdom would help many people. Her silent leadership and patience would go on to be a symbol for all who wished to make a difference.

It would be a step for women, to be seen as different in society. Hair painted down and alone rather than in a crowd. She was the center of attention, in a time where women were regarded as inconsequential.

In a world of expectations and social standards, it was time to plant a seed. A seed that would encourage women tired of being oppressed to take a stand and be what they wanted to be. It would be a painting that people, centuries into the future, would study and make note of for its wisdom. The painting would be beyond its time, and would mark the world for far longer than expected. Women have a power, and it is one that comes from within. Their intentions are revealed or masked through a smirk or a grin. They have a power that is special; at least, that is what she would say.

She called her the Mona Lisa, and she represented all women who were captivating, brave and true.

CHAPTER EIGHT:

TIGER EYE AND LILY

In a faraway land lived a group of lost wanderers. They were a tribe of fierce warriors, dominated by powerful female authorities and the Council of Nikawi. They travelled through the deepest of valleys and over the tallest mountaintops, all desperately trying to reach the same goal.

Since the beginning of time, before history could recount, a legend brought to light the idea of a sacred paradise that could be only found when the cruelest of men and the vilest of women could work together and find peace. Only then would their perspectives be opened up, and insight would lead them to a place where no darkness could break the shared connection and beauty of the spiritual relationship that men and women were meant to have. From there they would begin to heal the dead and rotting valley of immortality, and find peace with the assurance that their ancestor's sins were forgiven.

That connection had been broken centuries before, when man had ruled wickedly. They used women for immoral deeds and treated them as lesser, and now the connection was far from being healed. Their roots went back to centuries before, but one creation story in particular, stands out among all others.

Their creation story recalled a moment when the Sun gave life to his light child, and named her Waaseyaa. That night the Moon too gave life to a child, and named him Ohanzee, for he was born in the shadows. The two were very unique and desired to be together, but the light drowned out the darkness, leaving Ohanzee as an untouched shadow.

Waaseyaa tried to find a way to stop the light inside her from shining out, but when she couldn't, Ohanzee became enraged; he thought she was playing tricks on him. He was jealous that Waaseyaa was so beautiful and could be seen by the world, so he tormented her by forming into scary images and causing her fear to open a door for darkness.

In time her light faded, and she became cold and fearful; all of her joy and hope had been taken away. But what Ohanzee did not realize was that without the light, his shadow could not be seen. Without Waaseyaa's light to keep him alive, he soon faded away. His images and trickery would no longer torment the once shining girl, but the pain left her broken and scarred, and she was afraid to shine once more.

The sun became angry with the moon, and the moon too was angry with the sun. They vowed to stay apart forever, so when the sun rose, the moon fell; and when the moon rose, the sun left. The line between the day and the night, darkness and light, were now more real than ever, and the world was very sad. Soon man and woman came to be in the world, who were opposites, like the sun and the moon.

They were meant to be together and live happily, but eventually, the man began to overpower the woman to become the leader, and the world wept. It realized it would need to save Waaseyaa. Then, her light would shine brighter than the sun and illuminate a pathway to peace that could only be found if the two forces became one.

Through messages and signs, it tried to communicate this to the humans, but they misinterpreted the intentions. They believed Waaseyaa was a young man who was meant to shine brightly and conquer the "lesser forces of darkness" that were meant to serve him—the women.

The battles began, and the men and women fought against each other until no more strength was needed. The women were intelligent, and with their unity and will to protect each other, they won the war and took their place as the dominant gender. But where there is an imbalance, there will always be suffering and pain.

The women were unrelenting, and they punished their captives by imprisoning them and making them do "women's work" as well as difficult labour, with the threat of death over their heads. Decades and decades passed, and slavery was all men knew.

Isn't it strange how odd things are when they portrayed in the opposite light?

After Adelaine's spirit had left the land of the living, it discovered the mystics of the ancient prehistoric people, who had lived millennials before and roamed the Earth using the power of Mother Nature to guide them. They possessed a mystical power, and used the elements of the Earth to rule over the land and survive against any foes. She sought to learn their methods and find empowerment in self-awareness, so she became Elu.

She desired to help the people find the peace that could be achieved through harmony; to help them become enlightened. However, upon incarnating as a child in their community, she was struck with a terrible discovery. She was a mute.

Oh, how your heart hurts. You wish to help, but how can you, when you can't even help yourself?

Growing up under the care of the elder women, she saw many incredible things. They were beautiful and used their knowledge of the hidden powers to create medicine from plants, heal the sick with chants, and speak with spirits through dance. But despite their wisdom, they were foolish in their cruelty towards men, as they had forgotten the importance of peace between all people.

What good is wisdom if you lack compassion?

Elu tried to communicate her intentions, but not many wanted to listen once they learned that her desire was to help the men, the ones who had tortured them for centuries. The women saw their wickedness towards the men as punishment for past crimes. Working as slaves, the men got little to eat and barely slept. Many young women would torment them as they worked hauling supplies around or cultivating the gardens. One woman, Amaru, liked to beat young men with long branches of wood, and insult them by calling them pigs and lowly cowards.

Amaru supervised the men as they worked, and used her power as an excuse to punish the men and "give them what they deserve."

Elu often caught her in the act and tried to make her stop, to no avail. She didn't like the injustice occurring and wanted to prove that there was a way to find harmony again, if the women would just give the men a second chance. She was frowned upon by many for trying to help the other gender, except for a select few shamans who praised her for her courage and purity of heart.

Some days were far worse than others, and today, she recalled a terrible memory that was forever ingrained in her mind.

His tiny body was covered in an array of various colours of bruises. Tears streamed down his face as blows landed on his curled up form. His tormenter mocked him, sneering, "You are pathetic and deserve everything you're getting."

The boy tried to fight back, but the penalty for disobedience was far more severe than the punishment he was receiving for snitching an extra piece of fruit for his only meal of the day. Elu couldn't blame him, as she crouched watching hidden in her hiding place amongst the bushes; the men were all hungry and weak from malnourishment.

Amaru, the identified tormenter, soon grew bored and moved back from the edge of the woods and into the clearing that led to the wood chopping stations. Stealthily, Elu made her way over to the injured boy and helped him up. The boy grimaced but was able to stand with difficulty. Elu felt sorry for him and tried to reassure him without words.

He spoke to her softly. "It's not your fault. You're the only really nice girl in our tribe, and you always treat us with respect. We are all very thankful to you, even though we don't quite understand why you're so kind. Don't blame yourself."

Elu's heart had jumped at the praise, but her anger surged due to her limited ability to make a difference. She brought the boy, who called himself Ashkii, to one of the shaman elders that she trusted, Isi. There, she treated his injuries and gave him water and food, before having to send him back to the workplace. He had looked back before leaving and thanked Elu for her help, his eyes shining with admiration and adoration.

Elu never forgot instances like that, and vowed that she would do anything in her power to prevent more people from suffering under the wicked's rule. Thus, upon the rise of the Harvest Moon, she began her journey to call upon the ancient spirits of the Sun and the Moon to aid her in her quest to sway the tribe towards the path of forgiveness.

This mission had never been attempted before, as the people were afraid of what could come to pass if the higher spirits were contacted. Because of the influence they had over the world, a single wrong move could cause them to furiously strike against the tribe. But Elu was smart, and she was patient.

She first summoned the spiritual being of nature and rebirth, the Green Man. In the woods, as dusk grew closer, he spoke to her about all the things she wanted to know, as he already knew what she was meant to do. His face, made of leaves, expressed his ancient wisdom. When he spoke, it was a sombre tone that longed for the old times when harmony flowed through the lands. The Sun had sent the Green Man to protect any beings that lived in the forests, and now he would support Elu, as she would be the first to ever attempt to contact Luna and Sol.

Once armed with what she needed to know, the Green Man lead her to clearing in the woods that ended at the cliffside. There he instructed her to light a fire, which in her excitement she immediately did.

Then the Green Man summoned the millennium-old ashes of the Pando trees, for they symbolized the past. Next, he retrieved a willow branch for wisdom and a cedar branch for healing. Elu pulled out a strand of her short, black hair and added it to the pile of materials. She placed the four items in the fire, and it immediately began to emit purple flames.

With her spiritual voice, she repeated one clear statement, "I summon the beings of Sol and Luna on this night, to put an end to the madness that has plagued our Earth from the beginning of time."

Brave people are often the ones who either have the most compassion or the most hatred.

Light and darkness, beautifully contrasting, yet meant to work together. Luna in her ethereal form was a woman of allure and mystery, forever equipped with the knowledge of shadows. Sol was a man of fire and power, forever fierce with his wisdom of all things light. Because of the hatred between their children, they too were cold and distant with one another, each blaming the other for their kin's suffering.

They appeared immediately after they were summoned. They were Sun and Moon, but they manifested in an almost human form, in order to be perceived by the people of Earth. The two hovered before Elu and gazed down at her questioningly.

Luna spoke first, in a voice that was deep and commanding. "Why have you summoned us here, child? Need you our assistance with a matter?"

"You are the first human to call upon us; about time, if I do say so myself." Sol spoke in a pleasant voice, but the underlying impatience was still present.

The Green man explained her situation, and how Elu would like to speak with them manifested in her ethereal form, as she was mute in the flesh.

The duo was understanding, and allowed Elu a moment to meditate to project into the astral plane. Once in the spiritual plane, she explained her plan. She wished to bring Waaseyaa and Ohanzee together again, by having them manifest into human form on Earth, so they could be together without their opposing powers pulling them apart.

At first, the two celestial beings argued, stating that their children would never give up their power. However, when Elu stated that this would be the only way for this solar system to find peace, they couldn't argue.

"Ohanzee is currently staying with his aunt Venus. He hasn't left in many centuries, but he will come when called," Sol said.

"Mmh. And my daughter Waaseyaa is currently with my brother Mars, learning about the Martians. She's not far from Gaia."

"Very well then, child. I grant you my permission to summon my son. I understand your greater purpose for doing this and commend you for your courage."

"And I as well. I do hope you will be able to help my daughter from this curse, and bring peace to all the beings in this galaxy."

Elu was overjoyed that everything was working out the way she had dreamed, and expressed her gratitude through the language of the soul. The two beings granted her special privileges, for being pure of heart and soul. Luna promised that the shadow people would protect her against any dangers, and that she could summon them for help when needed. And Sol granted her the gift of fire, so that she could summon it to light her way when she was alone.

They say bad things happen to good people. But truly, it is the good people who experience the beauty and ever-fulfilling goodness that can come only from bringing hope to others who had been cast into the darkness of fear.

Her goal now was to find the perfect moment to execute her plan. Returning to her tribe after thanking the Green man for his help, she was greeted with the sight of Amaru. As she neared, she realized that Amaru was not alone; the entire tribe was guarding the entrance of their settlement.

Their torches were lit, and they were armed with a variety of weapons. She stood before them, unyielding in her courage, but apprehensive and confused as to what was to come.

One wrong move, and suddenly, no one knows
you anymore.

"Elu of Nikawi, you have been accused of heresy, treason, and insurgence. For threatening to disturb our ancient laws and bring power to our enemies, we hereby ban you from our council and exile you to the lands of Anyox."

You hoped only for peace, but all you did was start a war.

"And if ever you should return, we promise to put an end to your life. And if you ever, ever, try to overthrow our rule again by summoning the higher powers, we will hunt you down. You were born unable to speak, but perhaps one day, you will be unable to see as well, for we will not hesitate to make you suffer."

The people that took her in, and took care of her as she grew up, hated her now. Looking up at them, she could no longer see the strong women who taught her the ways of the wind and sea. The women who taught her to hunt and sow, to work together, were gone.

Taking one last glance at the elders, her teachers, she saw that most were sorrowful but unyielding. Isi was amongst them, and when Elu looked into her eyes she was surprised to see peace. Isi's eyes were filled with serenity and calm as she approached her young student.

She took Elu's hand in hers and spoke softly. "One day you will realize the truth. You are not what this world sees you as; you are who you have always been, a kind soul trying to make a difference.

And nothing, *nothing*, will stop you from trying to save others from the suffering you yourself have endured."

In Elu's palm, Isi placed a black medicine bag that held the last bit of wisdom the tribe could give her. She then handed her a sac filled with everything she would need to survive in the woods. "You are now armed with everything you will need. Do not be afraid. Trust your heart and follow the calls of the spirit and the ghost inside. You are never alone."

I am not alone, for I have myself. And when I get to know myself enough, I become my own best friend.

She had no place to go, but left anyway. She journeyed to far off places, biding her time, as she knew she had to wait to act. The further away from the tribe she got, the longer it would take for them to find her when she finally did what she knew she must. She trusted her heart, and it was telling her to learn the ways of the world first and find herself, before discovering the true meaning of harmony.

Find yourself, lose yourself, but never forget who you are, once you find that out.

Time is suggestive, as some days feel longer and others feel shorter. We can make time slow down by focusing on it, or speed up when we forget it exists. So when she realized a full lunar year had passed, she could honestly say that it felt like no time at all. Her hair was longer now, resting past her muscular, tanned shoulders.

She had lived amongst the shadows, who protected her from the dangers of the wild. She mastered her power of fire and used it to create a heat and light source. She mastered every weapon she forged, and learned the art of stealth and camouflage. Her reflexes were impeccable and her stamina was astounding. Alone, she mastered the ability to be in full control of her emotions, and she recalled every incarnation of herself and saw them each as one.

She was Eve for her purity, Naamah for her remorse, Cleopatra for her fierceness, Marguerite for her compassion, Salem for her fortitude, Adelaine for her hope, Leonardo for unconventionality, *and Elu* for her wisdom. She was ready. She was ready to find peace with who she had become, and wanted to finally bring peace to the people of this world.

The Blood Moon rose and reflected on the gentle waves of the water. Elu summoned the people of the shadows to protect her against any foes who could emerge from the depths of the dense woods. Other tribes had been warned about her. She was now known as Killa by the native peoples; they saw her as the human daughter of Luna, for her allies were the shadows.

On this night, she would summon Ohanzee and Waaseyaa and put an end to the madness once and for all.

As the day reached its end, she lit a fire with her hands, and in that fire, she placed the contents of the medicine bag given to her by Isi. Cedar, sweetgrass, sage and tobacco, the four most sacred plants. While all different and unique, they were magical together, connecting her to the spirit realm. She then took hold of her dark hair, and with a knife, cut it off until it reached no farther than her chin. She placed it all in the fire and stood tall before the violet flames that rose higher and higher until they were taller than her.

She called upon the spirits and they soon emerged, strikingly tall and beautiful in their authenticity. With her soul, she spoke out and reasoned with them. "You are our last hope. If you unite and make yourself known to the people of this world, they will understand that man and woman are meant to be united as one. If you become human, you can be together, without your powers hurting one another."

The enticing girl dropped down from her hovering position and approached Elu with caution. "You wish for us to be united once more? Are you not content with the power the women have? After all, you are a woman as well."

"I no longer wish to live in a world where the woman rules over man. I want the men to have a chance to have power, and live lives where they are free to do what they wish."

At this, Ohanzee too came down to meet her. "Are you saying that you wish this curse to break? You wish for Luna's reign to end, and for the men to rule in your world?"

Ohanzee and Waaseyaa glanced at each other, making a solemn agreement. Elu was confused as to why they seemed to be working together, while she had believed they would have fought. "I want to give the men a chance, yes," Elu confirmed.

Waaseyaa responded, and in that moment something seemed to change. She retrieved a pendant from around her neck which glowed brightly, embedded with her powers of light. "Ohanzee gave this to me as an apology for his cruelty. He allowed me to be in charge of who ruled the world, and I chose the women. Now, I will give this to him, so that he may give the men of your world a chance."

She passed the pendant to Ohanzee, and the moment it rested around his neck, it glowed ominously black. "Now the men will rule the lands of your Earth."

Elu was disconcerted by this arrangement. "But I thought there could be harmony. Why can't men and women share power and live in peace together?"

It was Ohanzee who spoke up. "There is no harmony any longer. When Eve broke the promise to the Creator, she shattered the possibility of the world ever having true peace again."

Elu was horrified. "But that can't be. Why? Is this world meant to be broken and filled with lies? Why won't we ever just be happy without our egos?"

"Because it is in your nature." Waaseyaa's response solidified the truth.

In Elu's distress, she turned around and ran from the scene, leaving the duo looking sorrowful and regretful. She summoned the shadows and they brought her to her old tribe. In the settlement, she observed the chaos. Around her, the men were breaking free from their old captivity, and overpowering the forces of the warrior women. They didn't see her, but she observed it all.

Years passed in seconds, and she saw how men established themselves as the more powerful gender. She vowed that she would find a way to bring peace, somehow, one day. She realized she was in a vision, and that the chaos happening was a foretelling of the future. She rose beyond the settlement, and in her ethereal form saw the events of history fly by. Women being used as slaves, witch trials against the innocent, suppression, women being forced to marry young, no speaking, no disrespect, and always, no matter what, staying under the man's power.

Some women rose up: Sacagawea, Jane Addams, Mary Wollstonecraft, Eleanor of Aquitaine, Golda Meir, Emily Dickinson, Sybil Ludington, Sor Juana Inés de la Cruz, Joan of Arc, and endless more. Strong women, who made prominent changes in society, often unrecognized and shunned by the men in charge. There was no place for them because they were not considered human.

Do you understand the magnitude of the suffering in the world, going on every day? It is unrelenting in its desire to hurt those who try to end it.

Elu saw what she had done, and cried and cried. She wept for the women of her world, the women who were all her descendants. She was ever responsible for the world's suffering.

It felt that no matter what she did, and no matter how hard she tried, she always hurt others. She tried so hard and got so far in her attempt to redeem herself, but eventually, it mattered not, for all was lost.

She tried to restore peace by going back to a time and place before the struggle for power became so obvious. But she realized that something that always was would be nearly impossible to change.

At least, not on her own. But who did she have, anyway?

With the strain of the shock and horror, her human body gave up on her. Her spirit left her body permanently and she was forced to enter another life that she didn't want to live. With the realization that she was the cause for the suppression of women in the eras to come, she didn't want to live with herself. She was in shock and her spirit, conflicted, entered into a life that reflected her sorrow.

CHAPTER NINE:
EVEN BIRDS FALL

The funny thing about pain is that, as soon as you experi-ence it once, you never forget it. All it takes is a single moment to change your life forever. Phone calls, gunshots, heart attacks, and falls. Accidents, diagnoses, letters and cell walls. People aren't invincible, no matter how hard they try to convince others of their power. One thing we all can relate to is that we're all broken, and have fallen from our self-made pedestals, our strong, tall towers.

Her name was Sarah Rose Noble. Today was the last day she was living, because before, she knew what love was. She had been young and fascinated by what the world offered, and what she could offer it, when she discovered her new path.

She knew she had a brilliant mind once, too, and relished in tearing through books with a deep desire to learn as much as she possibly could. She was a hard-working student, who strived for success in all areas of her life. But above everything else, she could dance as if she could fly.

Her teacher, Miss. Addie, had told her once that she had the grace and elegance of a dove. She had leaped and soared across the stages as she expressed her joy and hope.

She was fifteen years old when her father died. They got the call in the early morning, when it was still very dark. Her mother answered, and had yelled frantically on the phone for several long minutes. All she could remember was gazing out the small window in her room and hearing a buzzing in her ears. She was numb to the world, but not to the pain.

For a long time afterwards, she couldn't remember doing anything at all. After many weeks of trying to help her, most of her friends decided it best to leave her alone. *Give her time to heal.* People come and go in life, but they will never last forever.

That winter, she found herself wandering around the dinghy parts of town, not willing to go home to the sight of her mother in a drunken state. She approached the rusted metal of the rough fire escape on the tallest building around and soon found herself overlooking the bright lights of the city on the rooftop.

In her lowest moment, he came to her like an angel. Little did she know that he was only a demon in disguise. His mesmerizing eyes entranced her to follow him and listen to whatever he said. He introduced her to a seemingly magical potion that could enlighten her and make her feel like she was flying. Flying was exactly what she needed to feel like herself again, so how could she say no? She was foolish enough to believe that she could soar again. She was deranged enough to forget that the world would clip her wings once more. It was then, at that moment, that her world went crashing down and reality hit.

She was a sixteen-year-old fatherless addict who was failing school, had no friends, and was dating a lowlife, deceptive street rat. By the time she had realized what she truly did, she was already gone.

I am indefinable. The world screams loudly at me and marks me as its example. I am not merely human because I chose to embrace a side of me that is far different from the flesh and bone that we see. I am a free spirit, one that will soar high above the clouds after I die, and impact others in this realm through the quiet voice of a girl. I will not be caged and labelled as an animal would, because I am indefinable.

The entire world always seems to want to place labels on us, and dictate what we should and should not do. Society strives to put us in a box and make sure we follow all of its rules. Society believes that if we do not fit the standards or accept its ideologies, we do not belong, and are therefore outsiders.

Except some of us like to break the rules. Some people prefer to follow their own standards of success and, no matter what happens, be happy with who they are. In fact, some people are so undeniably different that they make their own rules and create a new trend or lifestyle that more people will go on to follow. *She was not that person.*

Then, there are the people who much prefer to follow the leaders, the ones who crave a simple life with little pleasure. These people find it easier to follow a set of standards created by people who are believed to be popular because everybody says they are. *She tried not to be this person.*

Finally, there are the true outsiders. The people who, no matter what, can't seem to find their place in society, because they have never known what it meant to belong. These people are the outcasts, the ones called loners or antisocial. These people do not belong to a certain group or cliché; they do not follow the stream, and yet they do not always try to stand out either. *She was this person, and this was her story.*

Days came and went, and she felt as if she was centuries old. She had moments where she wondered what the future would bring, and forgot that the past was already beautiful. She laughed at the little things that happened to her every day; sudden snippets of song ideas coming to mind, or half an hour of staring off into space dreaming of being able to fly. Her tragedy was her strength, and her willpower would eventually enable her to move on and let the hurt of yesterday fade away.

At one point she believed that her mistakes defined her. She had begun to believe that they were what set her apart from others, and that she was unique because of them. She finally had a title, a name that would prove that she was worth something.

That was before she realized that she didn't need a title or label to prove her worth. It wasn't until she was at her lowest point that she truly realized that words were nothing.

"I am neither an optimist nor a pessimist, as my mood changes and influences my opinions. In the same way, I am not limited nor categorized into a certain social class, group or personality. I make my own rules and my own truth, because every single person on the planet has a different map, and will find what they are looking for.

"As humans, we believe that we know what is best for one another, yet we forget that we are destined for different paths. At the same way that I prefer certain musical artists and my friend likes another, we all have our own truths, built on the foundation of our values, experiences, and limitations.

"It is by understanding ourselves that we can realize that what this world believes is irrelevant, and that we may only be truly happy and spiritually set free if we allow ourselves to be free in our pursuit of wisdom.

"I can say that without a doubt, I do not have anxiety, I am not depressed, I am not a perfectionist nor a failure, I am not a victim, villain, or hero. I am simply me, and for once, that is enough."

CHAPTER TEN:

LIFE I WISH WAS MINE

Staring out the window of the black sedan as it sped along the highway, she thought about everything that made life special, and terrible. She got caught up in the fantasies in her mind; reality twisted, and memories fragmented. The only thing she knew for certain was that the sky was grey, when it was once a beautiful blue.

The masked men in the front seats stared directly ahead, gaze unwavering and robotic. Both were dressed identically in black suits and masks, but one feature stood out as a stark contrast. Wide, circular goggles placed over the mask gave them the appearance of mosquitos with bulging eyes. If one looked closely enough, they would see that indeed, the menacing eyes pierced you with a livid, red stare.

Currently, B-03 was being transported to facility A-803, the location of the Revolutionary Future Observing Device, or the RFOD. For eight long years, subject after subject had been tested to see if they would be able to handle the power of all-knowing and all-seeing. Unfortunately, due to the intense mental capacity and will needed to prevent a total cerebral shut down into a catatonic state, no one had yet survived.

Around her wrist was secured a tight black metal cuff with blinking blue lights. Her dark blue attire made her skin stand out in stark contrast, but even more so highlighted the spidery patterns on the dark skin of her arms. Staring into her reflection in the mirror, she could see the artificial wicked green lenses surgically applied to her outer eyes, to enable her to have the vision of a hawk and motion detection within a twenty-meter radius. Everything felt cold.

They took her to a secret place, one far away from civilization, deep underground. There, she experienced horrors that could not even be described as simply immoral, for they were monstrous. She was pushed to her limits, never having a chance to catch her breath before a new challenge was thrown at her. She soon realized that everything went in stages.

On her first day, she was forced unwillingly to enter a maze, and find a way to escape before the clock ran out of time. She ran for hours, always seeming to end up at a dead end. And when she stopped to try to take a breath, the walls would begin to close in on her, forcing her to move on. She survived her first day with four minutes out of the eight hours to spare. That night, she slept in what reminded her of a maximum-security prison cell, except much colder and colourless, if that was possible.

What did you see? Did you see it, or was it just me?

On her second day, they placed her in a large glass tank that strongly reminded her of an aquarium. They gave her an oxygen tank and connected her to its supply. At least she knew they weren't going to drown her. When the water began to fill the tank from the bottom, she shouldn't have felt surprised, but something about it caused her to be exasperated. It was *freezing*. Her feet began to feel numb as soon as they had been submerged for over a few seconds. The water rose higher and higher and she felt the cold burn her skin. It wasn't ice, it was fire.

> *Like fire and ice, some people may seem warm, but later reveal themselves to have just been so extremely cold that you couldn't tell the difference.*

Waist-deep, her mind began to shut down. She was shivering so hard that one may have thought she was suffering a seizure. Her circulation was slowing down, and her pulse was weakening gradually. Shoulder-deep, and she couldn't move any longer. She felt so, *so* tired. The water was almost over her head now, and her vision was blurring.

She was completely submerged. The oxygen kept her alive, but hypothermia had set in and was doing its job far too effectively. Her mind was a mass of sluggish confusion. She vaguely wondered where she was, and *who* she was. She realized that she had not thought of her name in a very long time. Since she was a young girl, she had been identified as just a number, but she knew she was something more.

> *There is always more to every person than what we can perceive as outsiders. We all have a story to tell, and we are all infinitely unique in our differences.*

She was not aware that she had survived until she was suddenly awakened by a bright light shining in her eyes. Whispers floated around and she picked up fragments of conversations. She was lying on a medical table as doctors bustled around, making sure she had recovered effectively.

Apparently, she had scored in the fifth percentile of those who had undergone the second stage of testing. In fact, her score, the time she had been able to stay conscious, rivalled many of the strongest subjects that had made it past this point. She didn't know whether to be pleased, or horrified at what was to come.

All she knew was that for the next couple of days, she was being fed decent food and was lying in a warm bed with fluffy white hospital blankets. She felt relaxed and at peace, and made the most of it. She knew it would not last. She was afraid at what was to come, horrified even, but had grown accustomed to the fact that everything was out of her control. She was used to being an animal, and not a human.

When they came for her, she went willingly. She complied with everything they did, until they brought her to a part of the building that she knew would bring her nightmares. *Lupus Locus.* The door's metal plaque displayed the name proudly. With her years of strict education, she was certainly well acquainted with Latin, and the name terrified her.

She fought to no avail. She didn't ever speak, as she could not, so her silent screams affected no one. She was tossed into the room, and it was promptly shut behind her. The room was dimly lit, but she knew there were cameras in every corner, with men watching her every move. On the walls to her left and right were sliding panels that would open if activated from the control room. She knew what horrors lay behind them, and she braced herself for the worst.

She sat against the metal door, her head in her knees as she waited. She heard a beeping noise. Then, the panels were slowly slid open as the pressure was released. Snarling noises and heavy breathing echoed throughout the room. Paws on the ground, nails scraping, and eyes glowing. She heard them approach her and didn't dare look.

The room went incredibly quiet, as if every beast had left. Until, in one instant, they were upon her like cats on yarn. Their nails scratched at her skin and their terrible teeth tugged at her limbs. She fought against their heavy bodies until she had no strength left. As she made one last attempt to escape, she fell hard on her side, and the impact hurt her head terribly. In that strange moment between the initial blow and the aftershock of pain, a single word came to her mind. Kione.

Kione. That was her name. She finally remembered it, after so many years. Perhaps her humanity had been taken, but this small victory made her feel that she had taken part of it back. She wasn't only a number, she was a real person who deserved the right to live. She was invigorated, and the adrenaline made her strong.

She viciously battled the nasty animals around her, and beat them until they cowered at her feet. She stood up on shaky legs, and with determination set, she stared up into the right corner of the room where she knew there was a camera. With her eyes, she was piercing the ones who had tried to take away her humanity and the things that made her *her*. She stared with anger, determination, and passion. They could do what they wanted with her, but she would no longer go willingly along with their plans. She would fight until her last breath, and she would die as a person, not an animal.

Take my body, take my mind, but no matter what, you will never take my soul; for it is unbreakable under even the most trying of circumstances.

She had passed the third test. She had survived every horror they would throw at her, and now they brought her to the end destination. The RFOD was stranger than she had expected. It seemed too abnormal for this world, alien even. The device's surface was made of what appeared to be a black non-Newtonian substance. It rippled like waves in the ocean, and seemed to call out to her. It held promises that could only be heard by the few people strong enough to withstand its pressure.

The structure was like a globe, spherical, but almost *alive.* When she approached it, it was…attracted to her? The substance reached out to her, sensing her presence.

She was pushed forward by an armed, masked man, when she showed hesitancy to move nearer. Seeing no other choice, she reached out her hand slowly. The minute the substance made contact with her finger, it immediately began wrapping around her body like tentacles, pulling her in. She didn't have a moment to think before she was being rapidly pulled into its body. Everything was black for a moment as she was engulfed, before she emerged unscathed. Inside of the "being" it was light, but the walls were still black.

She looked around, seeing nothing particularly distinctive. In fact, it was quite peaceful in the belly of the beast. The walls whirred and spun around like a whirlpool. The creature was excited with the presence of a companion.

Kione found nothing threatening about this anomaly of a being, as she believed it was impossible that this device was purely inorganic. She was unscathed and safe from the men waiting for her outside. So she curled into a fetal position on the ground and slept, for her guardian was awake and ready.

As she slept, she recalled memories of her past, before she was taken. She remembered her mother, and how her soft, dark hands had held her as she slept peacefully and carefree. She remembered her younger brother, Fynn, and how his laughter made her heart burst with joy. She remembered school and playing hide-and-seek with the other children. She remembered being mocked, too. She remembered how they had laughed at her, because her skin was dark, her hair was curly, and her accent different.

Discrimination. Segregation. Domination. All wrong.
Freedom was a right given to all of us the moment we were
born into this world. We are all wrong for ever believing
anything different.

Kione remembered the past, lived the present, and saw the future. What she saw in the future broke her heart, as it wasn't the better world she had hoped it would become. In all of the wars, destruction, and evil, she still saw humanity. She was not so naive that she didn't understand the nature of humans; in fact, she of all humans had likely accepted it the most.

As humans, we have filters. And these filters we cannot shut off, for they are how we experience the world. Generalization, distortion, and deletion. We experience the world through sensory information and must process it in one of these three ways.

These filters are necessary and good, but they prove the flaws in our human nature. We form thoughts and opinions based on our past experiences and the morals imposed on us at an early age. Our memories and beliefs affect our decisions and how we see the world and others.

Generalization is a gift, for it allows us to draw conclusions from a lack of information. However, it also may lead to stereotypes, discrimination, and assumptions about other people based on the circumstances.

Distortion allows us to have imagination, but it affects the way we interpret situations and people, leading to misunderstandings. And finally, deletion is an essential filter, for it allows us to remove unnecessary information from our conscious awareness so that we do not suffer from sensory overload. Deletion, unfortunately, is one of the trickiest of the filters, for it also allows us to forget the things we thought would never be useful in the future.

For Kione, forgetting her past life was hell. And forgetting her past *lives* was an even greater catastrophic nightmare. When the deepest parts of her subconscious mind were awakened, she remembered who she had been, and was no longer afraid of the future. Whether she survived or not didn't matter anymore, for if she failed, she would have other opportunities to share her story with the world.

Kione spoke to the universe with her thoughts, and the RFOD heard her too. It released her back into the real world, where she faced off with her enemies. Every scientist and soldier in the room was confounded by her re-emergence, as she was the first to ever do so.

She used their momentary shock to her advantage as she fled the room and sought an exit. Fueled with the courage of the many beings within her, she practically flew out of the maze of a building. She was pursued, of course, but nothing could stop her in her hunt for freedom.

Twists and turns, left then right, up the stairs and down the corridors. In the twenty-four years that this organization had been established, never once had they the need to deal with a powerful escapee. Anyone who tried to stop her was violently shoved aside or experienced terrible injuries as a result of her adrenaline-powered super strength. Somehow, someway, with fate on her side, she made it out.

The brightness of real sunlight hit her eyes, and she was awestruck at its beauty. She had emerged from the depths of the Earth to be greeted with the beauty of the vast, open desert. She was alive, and she was no longer chained to this world's selfish desires.

She was finally untethered and released from her bondage as a captive. She was free to be herself again.

A shot rang out, and she felt pain in her back. She turned around to see red eyes staring at her: emotionless, expressionless, inhuman. Damage to the spinal cord meant unquestionable death.

She fell to the dusty floor and stared up at the beautiful sky. The sky was the last thing she ever saw, before she felt herself sinking deeper and deeper still, into the darkness of the daylight.

CHAPTER ELEVEN:
OCEAN'S TALE

Sailing gently across the falling and rising dark blue water of the great sea was a small wooden boat. Not so unlike one you may hear of in a fairy tale or read about in a storybook, except for one... small factor... The sailor had long since left the boat. When a sailor leaves a boat, there is no one to guide it or distract it. It sails freely, without the burdens of the world and the pressure of society. Up and down it goes, calmly gliding to its end destination, home.

Nerissa of the Sea was what she called herself. She was a wanderer, a nomad. She escaped the world to find herself. She was beauty and she was light. She was hope and so loved the world, for it gave her a place to roam.

She lived not for the people, but for what she could do to help them. In the depths of the ocean, she sank. Deeper and deeper still, she went. And when, finally, she reached the bottom of the murky depths, she felt peace.

Eyes opened. Blue water met green orbs, filled with serenity. She rested, her dark hair rising and falling in the soft current. At the end, she felt peace, but that was not without struggle. Her lungs had burned, fighting for oxygen. Her body twisted and frantically tried to swim up to the surface, but she was in too deep. Then, her vision had begun to fade, and she had no more strength. She heard blood pumping, and her body seized. The ocean was vast, and filled with wonders.

Her lungs stopped breathing, her heart stopped pumping, and her body stopped moving. Yet her mind was always there. Her eyes stayed open, and she watched the ocean as it changed. Time went by and blue water turned to black, and the once plentiful fish became scarce. Nerissa was utterly and entirely alone.

It was in this time of silence that she studied herself. Paralyzed and devoid of any distractions, she thought about what she would do, if she could do anything. The ocean was a terribly frightening place. Its darkness and stillness haunted the few souls who had ventured far enough into its home.

But Nerissa had grown used to its intimidating nature, and found peace in its complexity. For beyond the violent waves and biting cold was the home of many extraordinary beings.

She decided that if ever she could pursue her dreams, she wouldn't travel deep into the depths of the oceans or around the numerous wonders of the world. Instead, she wanted to do something different. She wanted to fly. She wanted to soar high above this world and see the places she had lived from a different perspective. She wanted to feel small, in a world that would consume her in its vast opportunities and uniqueness. She wanted to go beyond the highest expectations of others, break records, and shatter the idealisms of the world.

And that was what she did, when she overcame the challenge of fighting off the ones who had tried to drag her down and suffocate her in silence. Her innocence and goodness were not drowned in the world's envy, as she had the fortitude to become the person she wanted to be.

And for the first time, she had a hope of seeing beyond the currents, and she saw the sky.

CHAPTER TWELVE:

UP, UP, AND AMELIA

She gazed across the grassy terrain where her glorious plane was situated. Its bright yellow colour shone in the morning's sunlight, and she wondered how her day would go.

The thing about flying was that if you left the safety of the ground, you had to realize that the ride may get bumpy, yet the fun was worth the risk of it all. The first time she saw a plane was at the Iowa State Fair in 1909, after moving there from Kansas. From that day forth, she knew what her passion was, and made it her goal to pursue it with all of her might.

Once you find your dream, hold onto it, and never ever let it go.

It was in 1920 that her dreams of flying had truly taken off. She attended an air show in Long Beach, California, and the rest was history. After a short plane ride, she immediately signed up for flying lessons, and off she went.

Within months she was an aviator with her own plane, and she would soon be a woman's name that every person knew. Yet through every success and every accomplishment, there were struggles. She didn't fit in society, as she was not like other women. She preferred trousers to skirts and comfort to fashion. She dreamed of sharing the accomplishments she achieved on her own, rather than being a woman who sat idly around waiting for men's orders. She was beauty and grace, but she was also fortitude and of an unconventional nature.

Up, up, and Amelia.
High she soared and gazing down,
She saw the world's great, mad frown.
It tried to keep her to itself,
When all she wanted was to know herself.

In the deep beauty of the night,
She gazed at stars so wonderfully bright.
They whispered secrets and words of courage,
For they saw her potential and helped her flourish.

When days shone bright and skies were blue,
She thought of everything that made love true.
Her dreams were vast and beyond this world,
Yet she found a way to see them unfurled.

She travelled to destinations far away,
And lived a life that was always on display.
She accomplished everything she wanted,
Yet her final destination left us all haunted.

She flew and she fell and she disappeared,
Whether it be in the sea or far from here.
No one knew where she reappeared,
But the whole world silently cheered.

The world silently laughed and jeered,
For this put a stop to the women's rights revered,
She was lost from this world and drowned in the injustice,
As this world was cruel and filled with corruption.

Amelia glanced back at her navigator, Fred Noonan. The devices were failing her, and she knew her luck was running out. Sending one last message out, hoping someone would hear, they began their descent into the ocean. She was back to square one.

CHAPTER THIRTEEN:

THE QUEEN WHO LOST HER HEART

Perhaps it is not always about the battle between good and evil. Some say it is inevitable that the hero always wins, that they save the world and ultimately defeat the greater threat. But what happens when you fight the world with all of your strength, only to come to realize that the battle is within? Monsters live in this world, that it is true, but greater monsters creep up on us in the darkness, when we are misguided and being led from the light.

The minute we are distracted, our focus on building walls around us, the enemy is revealed to be trapped in with us. Or maybe the enemy is not always revealed to be around us or within us, but in the people we trust the most and keep closest to us. The line between good and evil is not clear, but rather faded and broken; the two become mixed and intertwined. And the best thing to do is to accept both and stand not on either side, but in the middle.

Her piercing black eyes stared, fixated on a point far away, among the snow-covered evergreens and sharp-pointed mountains. Pale skin shone as bright as the snow and her long, black hair whipped wildly against the steady winter breeze. When the sun rose in the early hours of the morning, it marked the seventh month of her reign of her late father's kingdom. Madame Lucille Fonseca was the Queen.

Lucille was a queen in this life, like many of her other counterparts. She was a parallel, yet an enigma. She represented the women who had ruled before, and had yet to rule. She was Cleopatra, Catherine the Great, Princess Pingyang, and Queen Victoria. Strong women who had marked the world with their iron fists. So when she said that the art of ruling was not new to her, she was not lying.

However, in this life, Lucille's struggle was not to do with inner turmoil or the unfairness of the world, or at least not entirely. In all of her lives, in all of her experiences, she had yet to experience true romance, and the fulfillment that comes with falling in love and being with a person who makes your world complete.

She had grown frustrated with society, and all the men who wished to court her for the financial benefits. For once in her existence, she wanted to be truly loved for who she was, and not only be consumed by the loneliness that came from losing people you love in every new life she experienced.

So, as ever the independent idiosyncratic that she was, she pursued the unconventional route and followed her heart. Her heart, it seemed, led her much farther away than she ever would have thought. It brought her around the world, from cities to slums, to riches and rags. She left her kingdom under the care of her youngest brother Aleksander for the time being, and explored the world herself for a while.

One year, in China, she met a young boy named Liang who taught her about the beauty of the rabbits. He told her about the legend of the *Moon Rabbit*, and how it was the moon goddess Chang'e's companion. He showed her his sketches and his interpretations of the legend. She asked him about one particular image that portrayed the rabbit pounding a substance in a pestle. Liang told her that this substance was the elixir of life.

Lucille asked him why the Chinese celebrated this legend in particular, as evidenced by the numerous children who had toy figurines of the rabbit dressed in mighty armour. The young boy told her it was because the rabbit had come to Beijing centuries ago to save them from a horrific plague, and cured them with his special powers. He had been humble and asked nothing in return. He symbolized hope, in a world that was dying.

"Where is he now?" Lucille asked, curious.

The boy's voice was excited as he spoke with passion. "Well, he went back to the moon, of course. He couldn't leave Chang'e alone forever!"

Later, Lucille thought back to the conversation she had with the young boy. In all of the centuries she had lived, she never once heard a soul speak about loneliness. It seemed to be something people always kept to themselves, or perhaps many never experienced it at all. She still questioned God's motives for this journey she was living. But, she had been more at peace with it since she died as Amelia, for she left behind a legacy and died with a meaning.

After her conversation with the young boy, she began to wonder again what the purpose of her journey was. And, ultimately, God really wouldn't leave her alone forever, because he loved all of his children and would only allow them to go through hardship if he believed they would make it out stronger in the end.

You know why I'm living, and you know how I'll die. But most importantly, you created me for a reason, and that's why I try.

It was on a trip to Bulgaria that she discovered the power of peace. She had been fascinated by the beauty of Eastern Europe, and decided to travel there to experience it first-hand. She loved its old buildings and enticing history, and its foreign culture and different people.

She met an old man, on her way from the town square one quiet morning. He asked her about her day, and if she was faring well, seeing as he could quickly guess she was a traveller.

She told him she was a nomad, travelling around the world to find the secret of life.

The old man barked out a laugh, filled with mirth. "There's no secret to life, I'll tell you that. But if you want to find some peace in this mad world, live a simple life."

"What do you mean, exactly?"

"Living a simple life means enjoying the little things in life, like watching the birds fly on your way to work, or watching the sunrise on your porch in the morning. It means being free from more commitments than you can handle, so you can have time to live in between them."

Lucille was curious and wished to understand more about the man with unexpected wisdom. She was also confused at his message, and somewhat affronted. "What are you doing with your life, then? Do you have a family?"

"I did. Many years ago I had a family, that I loved very much. But I also had a job that I spent too much time at. I didn't realize at that time that I should have treasured my time with those I loved, and made it a priority to spend more time with them every day."

"What happened?"

"I'll tell you the story if you wish, but it'll take a while if I do. Would you like to get tea, the bakery across the street is a good one?"

Once Lucille and the man, who went by Tihomir, were settled comfortably in the dimly lit bakery with steaming mugs of tea, he spoke. "I remember the last day I spoke with my wife." His voice was scratchy and he struggled to speak. His voice came out in gasps, and his old age was evident as he told his story. "Money had been an issue, so I worked all the time. Late nights and very few holidays took a toll on my family. She was angry that I was never home. She feared for our children, Andrei and Diana. We fought constantly when we should have treasured the few moments we had together."

"What was your wife's name?"

Tihomir smiled and stared out the dusty window as he recalled memories. Tears began rolling down his face as he cried in joy and sadness. "Her name was Anastasia. She was beautiful, and she was my world until I destroyed her."

"What do you mean? What happened to her?"

"One day, when we were fighting, I had enough and tried to leave the house to get some air. She was furious and followed me out. She had been distracted as she ran after and screamed at me. I made my way across the street quickly, but when she tried to pursue me, she failed to notice the approaching carriage. The horse was startled and violently lashed out, kicking her hard in the chest. She died immediately."

"I'm so sorry for your loss."

"Thank you. You are a kind woman."

Lucille passed him a handkerchief and gave him a minute before asking him her next question. "What happened to your children after?"

"I sent them off to live with their Aunt Olga, who was quite wealthy and could give them a proper education. What I didn't know was that my daughter quickly developed a terrible illness upon her arrival. When I found out and arrived at the home, it was too late. She passed away not a week later."

"And your son?"

"He lived with Olga for many years, and eventually got married. He hasn't spoken to me since the death of his sister. I haven't seen him in eight years now, and pray he is alright."

"I'm so terribly sorry for everything you went through. How can you be so strong, even though you went through so much?"

"Life isn't about being strong, it's about finding peace in the midst of the chaos. You don't fight the waves crashing on you, you let them pass and follow their lead, for they are guiding you to your next destination. It was hard, but eventually I found peace in all of the hurt, because I knew I deserved happiness no matter how ignorant and stubborn of a person I was and no matter what I went through."

Lucille thought about his message, thanked him, and bade him farewell. And she left quietly, pondering thoughtfully, for she understood the secret of peace. And she knew now that peace was attainable, even for those who live amongst the insanity of this world.

Two years later, she found herself in Peru, where she learned to live the way of the native people. She saw how they lived in poverty, in many isolated parts of the country. She watched as they lived happy lives, where family, community, and faith brought them together.

She found it curious how they could live with the constant risk of bandits and criminals stealing their possessions, and the fear that came from not having enough. As months went by, she realized that they didn't have to live in fear, for they were free. They helped each other, neighbour helping neighbour, true families. It was their fellowship that made them strong, and their optimism, their biggest virtue. Still, Lucille wished to know more, and understand the beauty of joy.

Sitting on the roof of her residence, she gazed at the tinted horizon as the first streaks of colour peeked through. The stars had long faded, and she missed their light, but soon it would be morning. The roosters croaked and soon the locals would be up, tending to their animals. And Lucille would go to school, where she would teach the children everything she deemed important to know. She loved her secret life, the one she made for herself. For in it, she could do whatever she pleased, until her kingdom called her back.

Amongst the many women in the community, there was one who stood out the most. Maria was a woman around her own age who took care of all the younger children when their parents couldn't. She took in orphans and those who needed a place to stay while their parents left for the city for business.

She reminded Lucille of her own mother, when she was Naamah, for they were of similar nature. She desired to speak with this particular person, and learn her story, for they were so alike.

She approached her early on that morning, while Maria was hanging laundry on the line. The morning was hot and dry, and the chickens scratching on the ground caused dust clouds to rise. She greeted Maria in Spanish, before walking over to her. Maria stood to meet her before inviting her in for coffee. They spoke about the locals, the weather and the crime rate.

Eventually, Lucille took her chance and asked her a question that had been on her mind since she moved to the country. "Why are you all so happy here? You struggle with poverty and crime, and yet you are all still so happy."

Maria smiled and laughed before speaking in a voice filled with a wisdom that only an old soul could possess. "Our secret is that our love for one another is stronger than our fear. We focus on the things we have, and the happiness we have with one another, rather than material things. We treasure memories and are content with the necessities, and we always have enough."

"So the secret to joy is gratitude, isn't it?"

"Of course. Being thankful to the Father is essential to good health, fortune, and joy."

Lucille thanked her friend for her wisdom and left renewed with a new vigor for life. Through all of her adventures, she had learned something from everyone she met. She had yet to find the secret of love, but she discovered the secrets of hope, peace, and joy. And with this knowledge, she pursued love, and found it not in the world, but within herself. The secret to finding love was to love yourself first, and accept every part of yourself, good and bad.

Lucille returned to her kingdom after five long years of travel. In her absence, her kingdom had not changed; in fact, it remained exactly how she left it. Her family was pleased to see her, but rather surprised at her arrival. Most believed she would never return once she discovered the freedom outside the castle walls.

Lucille Fonseca returned to her throne, and ruled her kingdom once more, but she felt that something was missing. For months, she roamed the castle rooms and tried to get used to a life of royalty again. But soon enough, she realized that she did not belong.

She imagined herself climbing trees in the jungle, touring the pyramids in Egypt, visiting the Taj Mahal, and hiking in the

Sahara Desert. She wanted a life where she could choose her path, and use her learned knowledge to develop a wisdom that came only from experience.

Her brother Aleksander noticed her melancholy and quickly realized the cause of it. He asked her why she wouldn't return to her adventurous life, for he knew she was happier there. She told him she felt guilty of placing the burdens of ruling on his shoulders, as she was the eldest child.

Aleksander told her his story. He told her that he always felt bad that she was the eldest child, because he knew that she never liked commitment as a child. She was a free spirit, and he wished he could take her responsibilities. But he was also afraid because of her stubbornness; she would insist that she could do it and reject his offer further.

"I'm telling you this because I want you to know that I don't have the desire that you do to see the world and explore the beauty of the endless opportunities out there. I have always lived inside these castle walls, and I have come to see them as my home. I will defend it, as I have in your absence, and am at peace with the burdens of controlling an empire."

Lucille was amazed at the wisdom her younger brother possessed. She asked him if he would be willing to take over her place permanently, should she truly leave.

"I promise that should you ever leave, sister, I would do my best to follow your brave footsteps and rule with honour and compassion. And because I know you, I will always wait for you, because I know you will come back when you wish to be reminded of the life you had. And should you ever wish to return to the throne, I will wholeheartedly step down and allow you to take back your rightful place as Queen."

"Then on this day, I surrender my reign over to you permanently. You will rule as the leader of this land. Thank you, brother.

You have been my best friend since I was adopted into your life, and I thank you for supporting me through everything."

With a final embrace, Lucille made plans to leave, and did so. She left to pursue her dreams, and didn't look back until her return many years later. For she knew, that no matter how far she wandered, no matter how long she was away, her home would always be waiting for her upon her return. She pursued love and found other gifts, and at the end, she came back and found rest.

CHAPTER FOURTEEN:
ORPHAN'S LOT

Marina stood across from him in the darkened parking lot, watching the way his ebony hair brushed his pale face and his soft yet dark blue eyes focused on the ground in front of him. With his hoodie pulled over his head and his hands in his pockets, he appeared to be hiding something, or perhaps up to something troubling. Yet something about the way he stood unmoving there alone, in this rather uneventful location, stirred up confusion and interest in her.

However, when the colourless theme of the scene was disrupted by the sudden bright light of a car pulling up, she shielded her eyes with her arms and turned away. When she looked up, the boy was struggling with what appeared to be an unexpected attack from the black sedan's occupants.

A large man gripped him with incredible strength and slammed him against the side of the car, yelling furiously in his face. While the words were impossible to decipher from her position, the danger of the situation was obvious. Overwhelmed with a spontaneous urge to help, she ran forward and cried out for the men to stop.

The minute they heard her they turned around, and a glint of metal caught her eye. Two shots rang out, loudly and threatening. Falling to her knees and shielding her body, she could just catch the movement of the car speeding away, leaving no one behind. Left unscathed, she picked herself up and stood watching as the lights faded away, leaving her once more alone.

Marina had learned at an early age that everything that makes us who we are is partly due to our experiences, but more so our choices. She wished to share this secret with the world, as so many were discouraged by their own past mistakes, failures, and hardships. Many believed themselves to be broken, but surely, we couldn't be truly broken if we had the choice to fix ourselves.

Even the thought of the belief that we could be healed was enough to transform us. For when there was but a small strand of hope, we had the choice to either grasp it with the full knowledge and understanding that we could use it to pull ourselves out of the deep pit we buried ourselves in, or we could grasp the rope and cut it off, falling deeper into the darkness.

This was but one of the millions of views on life, a mere perspective of a young girl who had, without a shadow of a doubt, used it to diminish any fear of the unknown.

At the age of seven, Marina had come to know a word known only as abandonment. Growing up in Indianola, Mississippi with a mother who made a living from dry-cleaning and a father who worked as a delivery driver for the town, they barely managed to scrape by. Living paycheck to paycheck and already being forced to use food stamps, the pressure of working hard was at its absolute peak.

Eighteen-hour days were considered average for the family, and minimalism was the key to survival. Seeing as hiring a babysitter was beyond their budget, Marina was always home alone after school. With no extended family to converse with, and no parents around to mentor her, Marina soon began to construct her own ideas of the truth about reality.

She believed that money had to be the most important thing in the world, as it consumed her family's entire life, and that you were only allowed to feel happiness if you achieved something great. She spent every waking hour of the day reading and vigorously working hard at studying, and anything else she believed would catch her parent's attention, be it cooking or chores. Committing herself to a life of hard work and independence, she began to buy into the notion that love too was a gift meant only for those worthy of receiving it.

In time, however, she came to realize that nothing she could do would ever be enough, and finally, on one devastating evening, she truly felt it.

Sometimes you have to feel it to believe it.

It was Friday, July seventeenth, her twelfth birthday, and her mother was working late, having at least promised to celebrate with her once she got home at eleven. Her father, she didn't know where he was, but she had a sneaking suspicion that he was at the bar, his recently declared favourite place to be. While she hated to admit it, the small family was slowly falling apart, leaving them more financially burdened than ever.

She would be a fool if she didn't notice the needle caps littering the ground around the garbage can, or the bottles stuffed under her parent's bed and the couch. If she had not been up in the evenings, she would have never heard her father come in with other women, but she always was.

If she hadn't been in the parking lot of Cafe 0 the previous month, she would have never witnessed her mother hooking up with the owner, nor would she have realized her mother's gambling habits. Despair was a word that would have described the sorrow she felt, but she was so used to it by then, she called it emptiness.

She tried filling that void by finding other people she could look up to and please, but teachers only saw her as one of the many other above-average students they taught in their career, and community members only saw her for her family's reputation. Once, she tried talking to a priest in her local church, but once he discovered her surname, he kindly stated that he would have nothing to do with her name and wished her luck.

She felt like an outcast, be it as the pathetic emo-nerd of the school or the useless Coleman's daughter. She was at her rope's end, fully intending to do everything in her power to ensure that it would not break due to her circumstances. Today would be the final test, the one opportunity she was giving herself to change everything about herself, and her life.

Her father came home at three a.m., stopping briefly to purge himself of his excessive consumption of alcohol, before promptly collapsing on the couch. If he had seen his daughter watching him from the hallway, he would have seen the devastated expression on her face and the stuffed backpack resting on her shoulder.

Another piece of her soul fractured. Eventually, it turned out that her mother decided to take the night shift that day, starting right before she returned home from school and ending the following morning at seven a.m., the time when Marina was out at the library. However, when her mother arrived home, she was not greeted with silence, but a distraught pre-teen at the door.

"Marina, what are still doing here, you shouldn't be here," she gasped out with unadulterated shock.

The way she carried herself suggested that something was off. Sleep deprivation and drugs, Marina surmised. She said nothing as her mother eventually broke the stare, took off her coat, and made her way to the kitchen.

Her mother walked to the sink, washed her face and turned around before asking, "Are you sick?"

Marina found it funny; she hadn't seen her mother in weeks, and once she did, the first assumption was that something was wrong with her physically. How very wrong everything was about her life. She observed, not commenting, evaluating her mother's every move, her decisions and intentions.

Receiving no answer, Ms. Coleman approached her daughter to feel her forehead but was abruptly stopped by a raised arm. "What's the matter with you, Marina?" she exclaimed, now beginning to feel irritated.

A cool mask of indifference melted into place on Marina's face. "Wrong? What could possibly be wrong when I live such a perfect life? What could possibly be wrong when my family loves and cares about me so much? What could be wrong when my mom and dad chose to be addicts and cheaters, instead of my parents?" She ended shouting furiously, making her anger fully apparent. Unfortunately, the loud volume woke up her father, amazingly she might add, and soon enough he was at the scene too.

"What the hell is your problem, you ridiculous child?" His anger made her fit seem like a casual conversation.

Her father had never been an angry man. Growing up, she had seen him as very passive and patient, always willing to listen to others. Watching the man before her now, she realized with a start that this was not her father anymore. She burst out in tears, too distraught and suddenly fearful at the outburst.

149

Terribly enough, the man who was once her father did not take kindly to this, and approached her with an expression equivalent to that of an angry bull. She stepped backwards, finding herself pressed against the wall, paralyzed in shock and horror.

The man wrapped his hands around her throat and shook her furiously, yelling at the top of his lungs. "We do everything for you, you ungrateful child, and this is how you repay us? Maybe it's about time you got a lesson in humility!"

The harsh backhand against her face stung something awful, and the vicious punch to her temple sent her flying across the room. At that moment her mother interfered, whispering desperate pleas and trying to convince him that the consequences greatly outweighed the benefits.

A gruff expression came onto her father's face and he returned a comment. "You discipline this excuse for our daughter then, just make sure to give her a taste of the real hell we were put through when she was born."

All she could hear was her mother's promise to do just that over the pounding in her head and the pain in her ribs as a result of her crash landing. Putting in great effort, she turned her head to gaze at her mother's traumatized expression. Her mother's eyes roamed over her bruised, too-skinny, pale body and her eyes filled with unannounced tears.

"My God. I am so, so sorry my daughter. You deserve so much better than us *monsters*."

She came and knelt at her daughter's side, and was suddenly helping her stand. "You can't stay here any longer. You have to get out, escape. If you don't this will happen for the rest of your life," she whispered urgently.

Marina could tell she was referring to the abuse she had just witnessed at the hand of her father. The next moment, her mother was pressing a bottle of painkillers, a large wad of cash, and a pocketknife into Marina's hand. Her mother retrieved her backpack from where is was cast aside on the floor and placed it on her back.

As she ushered her out the door, Marina caught sight of an ugly bruise on her wrist and suddenly came to a terrible revelation. "He's hurting you too isn't he?"

She pushed her out of the door and peered out at her from the nearly closed door. "Yes, but that doesn't concern you anymore."

"But you can get out too. You can come with me. Please."

Marina was so afraid, about to be cast out of the only place she had to go. She pleaded with her eyes, to not be fully abandoned.

"I'm so sorry Marina, but I can't. It's too late for me, and if you stay, you'll become just like me. You must go." She was closing the door quickly now.

"No, please. Mom!" She cried as the door slammed shut, and promptly fell to the ground. She couldn't believe what had just happened; she was cast out by her only family.

She would have stayed there, on the ground outside her home, until the neighbors came out. Everyone knew that the area they lived in was dangerous. There were many people with terribly evil intentions, and the area was notorious for high criminal activity, including murders and rapes. The group of men who just came out were now standing in the hallway staring at the girl before them with hungry expressions.

One man, with a face covered in terrible tattoos, mocked, "What's the matter, little princess. Are you all alone? I'm sure me and my friends could take great care of you, why don't you come with us?"

Marina immediately ran away from the apartment, faster than she ran in her entire life, because for once, it really mattered. Adrenaline led her to recall her carefully devised plan, and she decided to stick to it, seeing as her circumstances led her to the same outcome, her leaving the city. It took twenty-seven minutes to reach the train tracks on the edge of town according to her wristwatch.

She figured catching a train to another city would be her best bet. Luckily, the next train to pass there would have departed at 7:30 am, meaning it would pass at her current location at 7:47, according to the distance it would need to travel. Glancing at her watch, she realized it was already 7:46. It didn't take but a minute, until the train whistle was blowing and it was suddenly speeding by.

She ran along side of the train, not having anticipated it to be travelling this fast. She tried her best to keep up, trying to grasp one of the train car's handles. Of course, with her luck, she should've expected something terrible like falling and spraining her wrist to happen.

Cursing as she tasted dirt, she frantically got up, and despite the great pain, sprinted forward and leaped at the final train car, grabbing the handle and entering inside just before it was too late. Collapsing to the wood floor, she let out a sigh of relief before immediately passing out.

So close, yet so far from where you were meant to be.

When she came to, it was late afternoon. She figured after nearly two days without sleep and many newfound injuries, her body really needed to rest to recover. As she carefully got up and peered out the window, she was greeted with an amazingly shocking site. A beautiful lowlands landscape, so different from the concrete city she was used to. She realized that this train was not merely going to the next city, but the next state. This was Arkansas, no doubt.

She couldn't explain the sudden happiness that she felt, but she knew it must be because new opportunities were becoming more and more apparent. And besides, the farther away from her old home, the better.

She decided then that she would let this train carry her on until the very last stretch of land. For once, she fully allowed fate to lead her to where she needed to go, rather than taking everything into her own hands.

Sometimes in life, time seems to stop entirely. Such as during those quiet moments, sitting in silence, alone and devoid of any external influences. Those moments are the ones that seem to make everything you know seem irrelevant, unimportant, because you come to realize that nothing really matters but that of which you place importance on. Whether it be a career, people, other's expectations, or love, everything we come to believe is important is because of our choices.

But, if we lost everything, all the things that gave us purpose before, we wouldn't have any obligation, nor drive to do anything at all. And without that need, we would either feel purposeless, or free. For Marina, she was introduced to an entirely new atmosphere.

Minnesota, the final destination for the young girl clothed in broken promises. This was the place that the train ended, far away from her birthplace and family. Marina was not unacquainted with the street life, for she had spent much of her time wandering anywhere but her own home.

She saw the way beggars lay splayed across the sidewalks, not so different from the birds that picked what they could from one place, and flew away wandering to another in hopes of finding a new home. Now she had to experience this for herself, fighting each day to attain the basic, bare necessities of humans, food and water.

For the first time in her life, she could find true freedom being apart from the standards of society and as an outsider looking in on the world as she knew it. It was peaceful knowing that she had no more people to pacify, or expectations to uphold, but on one end of this very black and white situation, she was still alone.

Some people find refuge in solitude.

They see it as a way to escape the pain and evil of this world and get to know the peace that comes from within. But we all need someone, a person that is real, someone to believe in you. As children, we find someone to look up to and follow them, mimicking their behaviour. But when we have no one, we either find other influences or find our own way. People are too quick to assume that bad parents create bad kids, but in reality, we create ourselves by choosing what to accept.

Marina always found a way to survive, whether it be by dumpster diving, stealing, or going to a soup kitchen. She was a quick learner and soon discovered that living without rules was the easiest and most efficient way to get away with doing bad things without feeling guilty.

The first time she stole was during the first month of her living on the streets. Food had been getting sparse as a sudden flux of hungry newcomers invaded her city. These people were much bigger and stronger than her, and were far more desperate for food. The soup kitchens were crowded, and it didn't help that construction was currently taking place on the building.

The summer heat did little to comfort her rapidly expiring body. She could feel herself weakening every day, an occurrence she could not afford to let happen, as there were many hungry predators also searching for young, vulnerable girls like her.

So she stole; walking into the local convenience store, grabbing a pack of raisins and shoving it into her bag before discreetly sulking out. She had not wanted to steal, but she had not wanted to die either. So she told herself she wasn't stealing, she was taking back her right to live.

Many people wish to be remembered after they die. They want to believe that they would have made a significant impact on the world and others. The funny thing about death, however, is that people eventually get used to it, and they forget. They must move on, to prevent the grief from killing them inside.

And soon enough, what was lost is now simply a memory. After all, what is a body with nothing inside. It is but an empty shell, an abandoned home or a forgotten story with an abrupt end. There will be some who will be remembered for longer, praised for their contributions to humankind; but even they are forgotten. The saddest way to die, many say, is to die knowing you will not be remembered for but a single day.

Weeks went by, as they always do, and soon enough snow began to fall and autumn changed to winter. The cold was bitter and sharp, and eventually barely a single soul was brave enough to venture outside. Snowstorms grew unbearable and soon the city lights faded; the lack of power threatened many, as they had no way to warm their homes. Unfortunately for some, they didn't even have homes.

Marina was one of those poor souls who was forced to bear the cold. She went anywhere she was welcome: soup kitchens, churches, or abandoned homes. It was easy at first, because she would simply take shelter in any abandoned flat or house, but soon enough they were filled with other homeless people, most of whom were drug dealers or criminals.

The last time she had gone to a homeless shelter, the people in charge immediately tried to help her, saying that no child should be left alone on the streets. So she ran before they could call child protection services, and made sure they didn't get a good look at her.

Marina began to get sick shortly after. It was a deep pain in her lungs and the brutal cough made it impossible to relieve it. She spent many nights in whatever public place she could find that was open twenty-four hours, always alternating to prevent being found. Then, one day, as she was walking through an alleyway, she heard someone calling her.

It was during the early hours of the morning, about one o'clock, and she was rather shocked that she was spotted through the hazy air. Glancing up, she could see it was a woman calling out to her from the open window above. The streetlamp nearby illuminated the distance between them, and she could see that the woman was a nun.

"Wait there, please. Don't move, I shall be down in a minute dear," the boisterous lady called out, before shuffling about the room.

With no one to keep her there waiting, Marina debated on whether she should remain there as she was asked, or leave while she could. After all, the chance that she would be turned in to Child Services was high, and she would certainly not risk that, even if it meant being invited into a warm home.

But unfortunately for no one, the black, polished door slammed open and she was now in the presence of very tall, flustered looking woman.

Before she could utter a single word, she was briskly ushered into the apartment and guided into a kitchen, where she was promptly dropped into a heavily bolstered chair. Within minutes she had a blanket around her shoulders, a cup of tea in one hand, and a fresh pair of clothes on the table in front of her.

And through all of this, her newly found caretaker had not uttered a single word to her, simply ranting under her breath about the poor children of God being left in the cold.

As soon as she finished her tea, she was once again forced to make her way to another room, this time up a flight of stairs. She clutched her bag and latest wardrobe update firmly, much too confused and startled to say anything. They reached a small, peach painted room with a child's bed and nightstand at a record speed.

"Off to bed with you now, dear. We'll talk everything through tomorrow, but right now all you need are a fresh pair of clothes and a good night of sleep.

Suddenly too tired to argue, Marina slipped on the warm, cotton clothes and got into bed. She was asleep in a matter of seconds, the only thought in her mind... *When had life become so unpredictable.*

She slept on for a very long time, the warmth of the bed and the quiet of the home being the perfect motivators. When she woke up once more, it was not due to the stifling cold or violent activity, but of the stream of light coming in through the window blinds. For the first time in a very long time, she felt calm.

That new-felt emotion did not last long, as the sharp sound off a bell ringing sounded out. And as if the silence never existed, there were now young and noisy children bustling about through the halls and heading down the stairs.

This startled Marina, not only because of the noise, but because they were children, like her. They reminded her of her terrible days in school where arrogant, rich kids would mock her for being useless. With their loud movements and lack of compassion for others, as they simply rushed to be the first to get downstairs... the best.

Eventually Sister Mary Eleanor, as she was called, came up to have a nice long chat with her about her current predicament. Surprisingly enough, she asked little about her previous home life, simply opting to ask whether her parents were still alive or not.

Marina had prepared an intricately elaborate story to explain why she was an unsupervised child living in the depths of the cold-hearted city. She recounted her well thought-out story, which consisted of her father having left when she was young and her mother having abandoned her a few months ago, leaving her to the streets.

She explained how she had no place to go and was fully against contacting the authorities in fear of being placed with another less-than-stellar family, and therefore opted to fend for herself. Sister Mary Eleanor was far too naive and blinded by compassion to even have the sense to ask why she had been so wholly against being taken care of by another adult. Perhaps she was simply over-worked and tired, but she rather quickly left it at that and began making arrangements for Marina to live in what she now under-stood was a homeless children's shelter run by the Church.

Marina rationed that the Sisters here were all far too acquainted with stories of abuse, starvation, and the street life from all the children they had to take care of and were simply at the point of being beyond thoroughly investigating and rather opting to just help the newcomers adapt to their new lives as quickly as possible. With all of the rowdy and reckless children in this place, Marina wasn't very surprised.

Two months later and Marina found herself in no better pre-dicament than when she first arrived at the home. The other chil-dren were brutal, used to street living, and harsh in their assump-tions about any other residents that had anything strange about them. Marina, being the newbie, was a prime target for the bullies of the group.

Two older kids, about fifteen or sixteen years old known, as Brutus and Liz, were particularly cruel and cold-blooded. They called her freakish and worthless, and made fun of her quietness by calling her a mute idiot. The sisters tried to intervene, of course, but they were dreadfully busy, and often distracted too.

Marina spent her days reading and thinking, lots of thinking. Spring was approaching quickly, and she was hoping that as soon as the weather took a turn for the better, she would leave with the wind.

She got up one day, finding water in her shoes and sand in her clothes, another stupid prank. She was tired of being invisible, despite initially wanting to be alone. But her time with others taught her the importance of socializing, and now she couldn't bear having no one to talk to. That evening she packed her back and left a note, thanking the Sisters for helping her at the time she needed it most. She would now go back to her life of being a nomad; a lost wanderer looking for anything but a home.

Two weeks and many train rides later, she found herself in the busy city of Chicago. The change in scenery did her good, but what she was really looking for was a new opportunity. During her time as a runaway, she most certainly did not disregard the importance of education, and had spent much of her time at libraries, free museums, and galleries. She had searched for a long time to find one particular address, Stonewall's Correctional Facility for the Struggling Youth.

This particular school was a type of correctional facility and boarding school for young adults, and took any child off the streets that they could find and provided them with food, clothing, and shelter. The reason she was so adamant about finding this particular school was because it was the only one she could find that did not require a thorough background check of the students before admitting them in.

They assumed most of their students to be orphaned and homeless, therefore having very few questions to ask before admitting them. However, if they found out too much about Marina, they could very well discover the livelihood of her parents and bring her back there, not aware of the full implications of the action.

When she approached the fenced main entrance she was immediately spotted by a tall, silent security guard and escorted into the main office. She was then greeted by a rather severe looking secretary who began making all the necessary paperwork. And like that, she found herself several hours later in a comfortable dorm with half a dozen different uniform pieces and a timetable.

She was also given all the necessary supplies she would need for school, any necessary toiletries, and a card that would admit her into any of the school's rooms such as the cafeteria, library, and lounge. She had given a fake name, not wanting to risk ever being discovered. She chose her new identity as Marie Kohl, not wanting to stray too far from her given name. Finally, for the first time in her life, Marina Coleman did not exist.

Lone wolves are the people who are not afraid to stray from the pack, because they find peace in the silence of solitude. They look for life's greatest meaning, seek the mystical treasures found in adventure, and notice the peculiarities about the world that can only be spotted looking from the outside. They observe what others cannot see. They notice the battles fought within each person; the fight against ourselves. The outsiders are the ones who are not free from their own battles and the battles of others, but can recognize them and fight hard to find peace.

Marina met Mrs. Elizabeth Amarantha on the morning of her eighteenth birthday. She remembered the moment when she knocked on the peeling paint of the door of her childhood home. She had been hoping that by some chance she would be greeted by the sight of her tired mother or even the man she hated and loved, her father.

When she saw the severe, hawk-like gaze of the strange elderly woman in front of her, she was disappointed and relieved at the same time. Six years in the making, the tall confident woman she had become suddenly felt like a confused child again.

"Good morning, miss. I'm looking for a Mrs. or Mr. Coleman. I believe they used to live here," she inquired with no visible hesitation.

Before sparing her a second glance, the door was slammed in her face, leaving her staring at its pitiful sight again. For being not quite so unused to such an occurrence, it was one of the first times she had been thoroughly surprised.

She tried again, and again. Yelling and slamming the door furiously in her frustration. The door did not open again. Eventually she slumped against the wall next to the door, defeated and tired of searching for the people that left her.

Then the voice came as a whisper. "They're dead. You should know that, at the very least." It was the elderly woman looking down at her, having emerged from behind the door. "Your parents are dead. They have been for many years. I'm sorry."

She didn't seem very sorry at all. Rather, she looked as if she was trying to get rid of her as quickly as possible.

"Can you please tell me what happened?" Marina asked, forcing calm in her voice.

"No, I will not. I cannot. I am sorry, but please leave now or I will contact the authorities."

Her tone was clipped and her statements brief. She was unyielding in her request, held no pity and commanded complete obedience. This was the same tone Marina recognized in the many teachers and caretakers she had come to know. With the woman's tight bun, stern face, and grey hairs, it would only make sense that she had once had a career in education and strict discipline. But luckily for Marina, she was well practiced in the art of deceiving them.

"I was never going to find them, was I?" Marina spoke thoughtfully, disregarding the threat.

To her surprise, Mrs. Amarantha answered her. "That's the terrible part about it all. You were only a week too late to see your mother's funeral. She died of an overdose."

Facades crumble. When people are afraid or hurt, they build an imaginary shield to protect them. They become the person they believe will benefit them most in life. The person they once were is buried under the clay covering and as time goes on, they become less and less of who they once were.

But the sad thing about all barriers is that they can come crumbling down in an instant if enough pressure is applied. Whether we are old and bitter about life or young and already giving up on our dreams in life, we are all putting up a show.

We often spend years getting to know people; committing ourselves to the people we think we know and love. But we really know so little. If everyone's masks would come crumbling down one day and all the deepest, darkest parts of our personas became visible, we would never be able to function again. Truly it is the worst of us that brings about the goodness in others. Whether it be pity, empathy, or a desire to prove to themselves that they can be better, an individual's mistakes prevent the mistakes of others who come after them.

Mrs. Elizabeth Amarantha was by no means a kind person. She was bitter, tired, and impatient with others, especially young adults and children. When she first saw the young, boisterous woman on her doorstep, her immediate response was to drive her away.

When the girl refused to budge and first began banging on her door, she was furious at the insolent child and wanted nothing more than to send her off with the cops. And when she saw her sitting alone against the wall, her heart relented for the first time in many, many years.

She surprised herself by inviting the young woman in for tea, and once again when she offered her a place to stay until she got everything sorted out. Heartache was an emotion she was so well acquainted with, grief was another. But most of all, tragedy was her greatest friend and most familiar acquaintance in her lonely existence. And the girl in front of her fully emulated it.

Marina was very confused with the sudden change in persona, briefly wondering if the elder woman was bipolar. She would have asked some of her countless questions, but suddenly found herself very exhausted. She was introduced to the pristine guest chambers, and was invited to proceed to the dining room for afternoon tea should she awaken by then.

Not the first time in her life she was promptly presented with a place to stay, she didn't think much of it. She was asleep the moment the door closed behind her, and luckily, she fell on the bed.

Patterns of light danced on the walls around her, illuminating the flowered wallpaper and ruffled bedspread. The light breeze filtered through the half-open window and the distinct cries of robin birds broke the otherwise total silence. Spring, she realized. Spring was coming early this year. The scent of fresh lilies was prominent in the little room, but the smell of vanilla raspberry tea was more overwhelming. The thought of a warm drink to quench her thirst was a strong enough motivator for her to get up from the comfortable bed.

The walls were painted soft colors such as pale pink and peach blossom, much different than the disgusting beige it had been when she grew up here. Vases of perfectly fake flowers and expensive plates brought out the character of the home.

Making her way through the beautifully delicate home, she noticed the lack of pictures on the walls. Rather, in the places where pictures should have been, there were completely blank canvases disturbed only by a single splatter of black paint in each.

The tiny sitting room was decorated with an array of plush pillows and dainty tapestries. Something about the room was too delicate, too perfect, as if it were missing something. Mrs. Amarantha sat cross-legged, sipping her tea, with a weekly magazine in her hand. She noticed the shadow pass when Marina crossed the threshold of the hallway and looked up with a thin-lipped smile.

She wore a white blouse and a patterned skirt, as well as a blush cardigan that reminded Marina of an old antique shop. Her brown shoes were polished, but the ring on her finger looked old and worn. She seemed to be in a serene mood, yet guarded all the same. Nonetheless, she called Marina over and poured her a delightfully scented cup of tea.

They conversed about trivial things for a while. They talked about the weather and the town's latest news, both skirting around the topic they knew would be inevitable. Eventually, Marina brought it up, asking for an honest explanation about the events occurring regarding her disappearance many years ago.

The elderly woman instantly looked a decade older and sighed the type of noise that one would expect coming from a person about to relive the tragic tales of their past. Marina sat patiently waiting, but as one would expect, was entirely apprehensive and nervous at the thought of finally discovering the truth.

"There was talk after you had disappeared from the area. No one questioned it until you had been away from school for several days without any explanation. The police were called in to investigate after that. Many suspected it was your parents who had been responsible for your disappearance. But your parents convinced the court that it had been you who chose to run away."

"Did the police ask why my disappearance wasn't reported sooner?"

"They didn't have to. With the state they found you father in, they were certain he wouldn't have been coherent enough to talk, let alone realize you were missing. He was sentenced to prison for twenty-five years for illegal drug usage and domestic violence."

"And my mother?"

"She reasoned that you were a troubled child and that she always worked night shifts. She promised she only saw you on the weekends, while your father looked after you throughout the week."

"So she threw him under the bus to save herself, then?" Marina scoffed.

"In a way she did, I suppose. But you must understand that she was also suffering under physical abuse at the time, and wanted nothing more than to get rid of her husband."

"Then why didn't she just say that? She could have gotten rid of him for good."

"Because if she confessed that your father had been abusive, they would have had enough leverage to prove that you were being abused too and your mother didn't do anything to stop it. She would have gone to prison as well, and you would have been tracked down."

"But, what are you saying? I went missing, of course they would have looked for me. What case of a missing twelve-year-old girl gets brushed aside?" Marina was shocked and downright disbelieving in the face of the truth. But a part of the puzzle was missing.

"You see Marina, they didn't really have a reason to go looking for you."

"Why not?"

"Because you were already believed to be dead."

Silence rang through the stillness of the room. Not a single soul moved a muscle.

"What!?" Marina shouted breaking the ever-present quietness.

Mrs. Amarantha pulled out an old, brown newspaper from the depths of the deep drawers in the coffee table. "The night you ran away, you witnessed something awful, didn't you Marina? You witnessed a murder."

Marina did recall the night so many years ago. The forgotten, changed, warped memory. The terrible memory that her twelve-year-old mind could not process in the midst of all the traumatic experiences, so she deleted it. She could remember the boy, young, yet still many years her senior. She remembered the two vile men, and the two shots that were fired. But that was all.

"You remember so little, yet experienced so much." The aged woman was watching her closely, and surprised Marina with the tears that had gathered in her eyes. "I'm going to help you remember Marina. I'm going to help you realize what really happened." Her voice was quivering, yet firm in determination. She stood with an immediate aura of intense authority and motioned for Marina to follow her.

Marina was led into her old bedroom and was shocked with the familiarity of it. Nothing had changed about the room: her single bed with gray musty sheets was in the exact same position as the last night she had spent here, and the clothes in her closet were just as she had left them. The only difference was the walls.

The damp walls were lined with rows of newspapers, pictures and articles, all that were accumulated over the past six years and which were all concerning her whereabouts and the incident that day.

She ambled around the room, stumbling and taking everything in. She saw two newspapers, titles: "*The Mysterious Disappearance of Marina Coleman*" and "*The Tragedy of Marina's Murder.*" The memories were coming back to her quickly now, but something, no, someone was missing from the picture. Turning to look at the opposite wall, she came face to face with a picture of the blue-eyed boy. Attached to the picture was yet another newspaper, this one titled, *"The Tragic Deaths of William Amarantha and Marina Coleman."*

Last Sunday morning, the body of William Amarantha was found in an abandoned parking lot by a group of boys biking in the neighborhood. He appeared to have been beaten severely and then shot in the chest, before succumbing to death by blood loss.

The whereabouts of his killer are unknown, but the local police are doing everything in their power to investigate the cause of the murder. With less than twenty-four hours in between the disappearance of Marina Coleman, many wondered if the two incidents were linked. With further investigation, a shocking discovery was made. It appeared that young Ms. Coleman was on the scene at the time of the murder and was likely spotted from afar. The initial discoveries suggested that the young girl was likely taken hostage for witnessing the scene, to prevent her from telling an adult about the occurrence.

Unfortunately, upon further research, Marina Coleman's DNA was found on the scene and suggests that she was likely taken hostage as well. Without a body present, the case cannot be officially closed, but Head Detective Inspector Mark Jones stated that, "The case was futile, and the only conclusion was that the girl was at the wrong place at the wrong time."

He further advised parents to set early curfews for their children and warn them to be cautious of the nighttime activities of our increasingly violent city. It is the council's hope that the tragedy of William Amarantha and Marina Coleman will remain as a reminder to all, to treasure those that you love the most.

Further investigations will be taking place within the next year in hopes of further information being discovered about the reasons behind the murders.

Nothing in her life had ever felt as surreal as this moment. It was like floating in the air and drowning in the sea at the same time. She began to remember.

She was running, running and running. She was running away from the people who once promised to love her, and then broke her. Darkness. Darkness is a theme known to many people. It is the ever-occurring experience that we all come to know one way or another. Whether it be through loss, heartbreak, trauma or pain, it is the one thing that promises to be there, shielding us from the blinding lights of the world and choking us in its ever-possessive hold.

Making it out of the apartment, she made her way through the dark alleys and filthy streets in the neighborhood. She constantly glanced around, somehow fearing she was being followed. Unarmed and alone, she was a child in a large world filled with creeping, crawling and vicious monsters. The shadows moved around her, seemingly encircling her as she tried to find her way in the dark.

She heard aggressive, shouting voices in the background. Nothing was familiar about the town she grew up in. She had walked into another dimension, one where the loving hold of a mother or the gentle reassurances of a father did not exist. She had unlocked the door to a reality where humans lusted over money and destroyed their minds with substance abuse. She was a lamb in a world of hungry wolves, innocent and pure enough to hope that somehow, there was good in others.

She found herself in a quiet alleyway, illuminated by a flickering streetlamp. She sat hunched over, head in her knees, lost and wondering what to do next. Footsteps approached from behind her, uneven and stumbling. Gruff voices cackled and jeered, sounding slurred and maniacal. She felt paralyzed by fear, as the voices tore through the silence of the night.

"Hey, Clint. Look at the little sunshine that came to make our night."

"Don't be ridiculous Jax, the kid barely looks like ten."

The men argued for several minutes; they talked about foreign things that sounded disgusting and wrong to Marina, but she was too afraid to run. She was still frozen in shock, barely able to process all of the events of the day. A third party entered the scene, this voice far more authoritative than the last.

"What the hell do you two think you're doing? You both know age doesn't matter in our line of work; we pick up any kids off the street and take 'em to Shiv's den."

"Sorry Den, 's been a rough night."

"Well 'course it's been, with you lot drinking like a pair of blubbering fish. Now get to work, we'd better have at least three of these brats to show for next week and if not, you know I'll have both of you turned in."

Then the hands were there, gripping her shoulders and ushering her into a large white van. Feeling panicked, she began to struggle and shout, yelling at the men to let her go. Then, as quickly as it started it stopped, and the hands released her, letting her fall to the ground with a thud. She lied on her stomach and looked back observing the scene before her.

A boy, barely seventeen of age, was wrestling the other men on the ground. He caught her gaze and yelled at her to run away. She got up quickly and started sprinting away as quickly as she could. She ran until she reached a parking lot about a mile away. She turned around to look back and was shocked that there was a person watching her from across the lot. It was the boy who had saved her. She stared at him and thanked him with her eyes.

Then the shots fired, and she was startled to her very core. She stumbled, falling to the ground to protect herself. Another shot fired, and she cowered in fear. The edges of her vision grew fuzzy, and as she looked back one final time, she only saw the fading lights of the van driving away, before she could see nothing left at all.

When she came to, she realized she was lying in the same place as when she passed out. She surmised that not much time had passed since she had almost been kidnapped. She vaguely wondered why she was still alive.

Perhaps, in the poor lighting of the early morning, the men had overlooked her small body lying on the cold concrete and took the boy instead. Looking around, she confirmed that he was not there, and she mourned for the loss of the person who had sacrificed himself to save her. It was nearly dawn and she was tired, so she went to the station. The train brought her to a place far away, and she vowed that she would leave behind everything she knew about her past life, and move on to a new one.

"Oh my God. I remember now." Marina's heart pounded and chills racked her body as she relived everything from the flashback. "It was your son. He was the one that saved me."

Mrs. Amarantha watched her with a sombre expression. "Yes, he did. And for a long time, I was angry that you had lived and he had died."

"But, how did you know I was alive? Everyone believed I was dead, right?"

The old woman chuckled and let out a low groan. "Oh yes, everyone believed you were dead. But I knew better. My son would stop at nothing to help others. He would have made sure you had gotten away."

Marina stared into her cup of cold tea, and thought about many things. "Who was he? Who was your son?"

"*My son.* My son was an ordinary person, but he fought for peace. He was severely bullied growing up, you see, his father was abusive."

"I'm so sorry to hear that. What ended up happening to him?"

"I found out about it pretty soon after it started. I tried to force him to leave, to save my family."

"Were you able to?"

"Oh yes, I was able to make him leave. Permanently. But he took something of mine, something that I could never get back."

"What was it?"

The elder woman got up and made her way to a dresser. She opened the top drawer and took out a wooden picture frame that looked years old. She then returned to her seat and showed Marina the photo.

The photograph was stained and dirty from spending years in the drawer. It was a family picture, with a mother, and father, a son, *and a daughter.*

The girl was slightly younger than her brother, practically a baby. She was beautiful. *Was.* Marina regretted to ask the question, but did anyway. "What happened to her?"

"On the day I found out that my husband was hurting my son, I decided it was time he left for good. He always seemed like the perfect man, responsible and hard-working, but on that day I saw a different side of him."

Marina watched as her companion took in a deep breath and continued, her voice shaky.

"We fought, as was expected. He didn't take kindly to the idea of leaving, saying it was his house and his children. I wouldn't have it with him, so I threatened to call the cops if he didn't leave immediately."

"And then?"

"He went insane. He grabbed our daughter from her crib and threatened to take her with him, so I could have our son. He said it would only be fair if we each took a child. Of course, I refused, and went to the phone. He grabbed me and pulled me away from the phone, violently. I was so shocked that I did the only thing I could think of, grabbed the steak knife from the sink."

Marina was holding her breath now, fearing the end of the tale, but needing to hear it anyway.

"I went at him with it and got him hard in the gut. I remember his scream like it was yesterday. He had still been holding our daughter, but when I stabbed him, he dropped her. The impact on her head killed her instantly."

Marina ended up going to the silently weeping woman and comforted her as she struggled to finish.

"I watched him bleed out, our daughter dead beside him. My son and I held each other as we stood horrified at the turmoil that had become our lives. I was so sorry that I hadn't realized what was happening sooner, but my son said he never blamed me anyway. Court trials took place, and eventually, I was cleared for the murder. After the ordeal, however, not many people were willing to hire me. My son and I mourned, and suffered from PTSD. He was bullied in school, and I could do very little as I had to work making fabric every day."

"Weren't you compensated for your husband's death?"

"Funny thing was that we were, but we barely had a chance at using any of the money before it got stolen by my sister-in-law. I didn't want to go to court again, because it would take even more time away from my son, and I didn't trust anyone to look after him."

"How did your son manage to survive all of this?"

"My son was extraordinarily bright, and had always cared for others. He was bullied because he helped others who were mocked for being different. He was optimistic, even after all the horrors he suffered. I wish I could have been as brave as him, and I wish I could've been a better mother."

"You did everything you possibly could. The world was unfair, but you did the one thing that he truly needed; you loved him with all of your heart."

"Oh Marina, if my daughter was alive, I would've hoped she had turned out something like you. You and my son are so very similar."

"Perhaps we could fill the void in each other's lives, and help each other move on?"

Mrs. Amarantha truly smiled for the first time then. A light filled her eyes and she looked and felt hopeful for the first time in years. "Marina, I want to adopt you."

Those six words changed the young woman's life forever, and she thanked the God up above that no matter how terrible life could be at times, there is always hope for a future with love and forgiveness.

They lived, they loved and they lost. But they conquered the world, because they forgave. They forgave, not forgetting, and moved on to a new chapter. A new chapter where the orphan met her mother.

CHAPTER FIFTEEN:
MOTHER OF US ALL

She experienced true birth in the year 1910. She had been thrown eighty years into the past, and became someone who had not existed before. Time was flexible, and she bent reality every time she lived a new life. So when she came to a complete understanding of everything on her fourth birthday, when she would have manifested in this time, she had no idea who she would choose to become.

She was born in the Ottoman Empire to a loving family, and grew up with the memories of her past lives resurfacing, bit by bit. Her father passed away when she was at an early age, so she once again experienced only living with a caring mother. She grew up knowing she was loved, and embraced the fact that her time as growing up as an orphan had passed.

Marina had lived an abundant life after being adopted by Elizabeth Amarantha, something that had been foreign to her. She proclaimed herself to be alive and disproved all claims that she had been killed. She was convincing, and managed to save her imprisoned father from further persecution. At the age of twenty-five, she became a lawyer, and quickly grew in popularity.

She became wealthy, and with her riches, she blessed others. Together with her adoptive mother, she created an organization to help troubled youth and the orphaned children of the country. She never got married, but loved every moment of her life, for she devoted it to helping children like her.

She was devastated when her mother passed away, but was able to move on knowing that it was a blessing that she had ever got to know her. When she was forty years old, she adopted a young girl named Ana, and loved her with all of her heart. She passed away at the ripe old age of eighty-nine, happier than she had ever been.

Now, in this life, she got to experience what it was like to have biological parents, and grow up being cared for entirely. She chose to become closer to God, and live a life devoted to Him. At eighteen, she joined the Sisters of Loreto. Within a couple of years, she was settled in as a nun and the headmistress of a school in Calcutta.

She lived a life clothed in humility and compassion. She sought to help those less fortunate and lead through example. She made it her goal to do the right thing and always be patient. And above all, her secret weapon was love.

In the early morning, as the sun began to rise, the air was dewy and the world quiet. She began her morning as any other, in prayer, before strolling through the gardens in the school's yard. The birds were softly chirping and the plants were thriving. She had taken on a new name, in her commitment to devote her life to God. Now, she was St. Therese of Lisieux.

She recalled the events of the past few years, and smiled a sad smile in thought. While she was always an optimist and one who strived to live with hope, she had experienced her fair share of trauma. The Bengal famine of 1943 struck the nation hard, and affected people everywhere. Teresa chose to live amongst the poor, rather than help from a far distance. She completely embraced their way of life and lived with nothing. In time, her efforts were noticed, yet the war raged on.

Violence between the Muslims and Hindus was raging, and division was a major issue. Centuries go by, and we are still the same. Humans may learn more and develop new technology, but behind all of the masks we wear, our nature is always the same. The thing about humans is that in every time, in any circumstances and in any place, we can always be counted to do the one thing we were never meant to do; sin. It is something that is in our nature, and it cannot be changed. Few people even come close to being truly holy, but few also try.

In this life, she strived to do her best to lead by example. She strived to help others help themselves, and be a worker of light. And even when times were tough, she stood by her promise: that she would always stay true to what was good, and righteous and kind.

The hurt cry out and the lonely never win.
The angry shout and the saddened are filled with tears.
In the midst of all that is wrong and terrible,
There is but a hope for the people of sin.

CHAPTER SIXTEEN:

MEET ME AT THE END

One day. One day is all it takes to change your life. One day is all it takes to experience the moment when everything you ever knew shatters before your very eyes. One day is all it took for me to realize…that reality was not on my side.

The game of life is one in which anything is possible, and every figment of your imagination can be brought into reality if you so believe. Unfortunately for many, their conscious mind is clouded with the distractions of the so-called "matrix." Infinite possibilities, multiple realities, a shift in consciousness and a transition to another dimension is all it took for me to realize this fact.

We often go about our days in a frenzy, and our days are often a collection of frantic moments where stress levels are high and our energy is being drained. We become so absorbed in the business of this world that we forget to seek peace, something that only comes from within when we are fully immersed in silence.

Bittersweet mornings and nostalgic evenings, and yet everything is so surreal. Life seems to slow down when you take a minute to sit down and observe the wonders of the universe. It is in these moments that we can ask ourselves the questions: what do we truly believe? At our very most inner core…who are we?

For some, they will say God's children. Others will say they are an infinite spiritual being. Some believe in reincarnation, Heaven, or both. And of course, with everything, there will be those who just don't know. And that's okay, because everyone will have their time.

I have decided to take my spiritual journey into my own hands now. I believe that a man or a woman can only truly find peace when they rise above the limitations of this world and take responsibility for their own happiness, and fulfillment.

In every religion, there is always some kind of reflection and time for growth, whether it is prayer, meditation, or ritual ceremonies. We are all trying to become the greatest version of ourselves. Faith is a beautiful thing that we should treasure dearly, however fulfilling society's expectations is often our priority.

In my humble opinion, rising above definitions or declarations of what is morally or religiously correct will bring you the greatest opportunity to develop your character, find where you stand, and begin your real-life journey. Beliefs will vary, but every belief system has truth to it. If we combined the knowledge of people everywhere, who is to say that we wouldn't discover a new revelation as the race of humankind.

There are greater things out in our universe than us. If the universe was a person, our galaxy would be the tip of its fingernail. We must not be fooled into believing that we are superior beings. Far too many unexplained and often supernatural occurrences have come as a result of our ignorance.

When we are ready, the creator, or to some Father God, will reveal to us what we need to know. But we must be willing to dedicate our effort to transitioning into this state. Much like a radio, we must tune in to a specific frequency to get the information we need. Where our attention is, so is our intention and mission.

It is the year 2074, and I am no longer what I had once been. I am not human, and neither are you. I am a multi-dimensional being that lives in a universe of endless possibilities and no limitations. Your planet Earth has been infiltrated by evil forces you call demons, from the beginning of time.

Other planets received the distress signal Earth sent out, when the nuclear bomb went off in 1945. We have been sending lightworkers to help bring peace to your Earth from the beginning of time, but have increased this number drastically.

You may recognize some of the most prominent lightworkers in history as Jesus of Nazareth, Mahatma Gandhi, Mother Teresa, and many more. The end of time is approaching soon. The universe is in the Father's hands, and he holds it steadily as its contents rumble. Soon, you will be free from the veil of sin covering your consciousness. Wake up. *Wake up.* Join the people of light as they bring hope and peace to the world. Fight the spiritual battles and dare to dream.

I once lived lives that hurt me with heartbreak, loss, and madness, but I overcame the challenges to find myself. Through the maze of life, the loss of my sanity and the countless suffering I experienced... I have discovered who I am beyond the flesh. I live not in fear that the Creator does not love me, but in gratitude, for He allowed me to go through struggles that made me strong. I understand pain, and beauty, and devastation, but I am at peace.

I have found harmony within myself. I make it my goal to help others find security in their own power, and the power of the Most High within them. We are infinitely blessed, and have no limits but the ones we place on ourselves. I pray for all my fellow brothers and sisters that love will meet their souls and they will be awakened with a passion to do what is good.

I know my place, and one day you will too. This is your journey, and mine, for we are one. I sign this transmission off with the only name I see fit... Eve. For first there was Adam ... and then there was Eve.

ABOUT THE AUTHOR

Laura Kostwinder started writing at a young age and is inspired by her mother and other strong women. She was born in Vlaardingen, The Netherlands before immigrating to Brazil and later Canada. As an International Baccalaureate student, it was a school project that inspired her to write her first book. It is her dream to become a successful author and share her vision with others. Through writing, she finds a way to communicate her ideas and by travelling the world, she has come to appreciate diverse cultures and unique people. When she graduates from high school, she plans on studying to become a doctor, while pursuing a career in writing. She aspires to help other girls her age and all people alike to realize the unique power we have within to choose light or darkness, and to pursue our deepest passions.